PEANUTS
MUSIC
Activity Book
An Introduction to Music

Compiled and Edited by
Sharon Stosur

ISBN 978-1-4950-5021-3

7777 W. BLUEMOUND RD. P.O. BOX 13819 MILWAUKEE, WI 53213

© 2015 PEANUTS Worldwide LLC
www.snoopy.com

For all works contained herein:
Unauthorized copying, arranging, adapting, recording, Internet posting, public performance,
or other distribution of the printed music in this publication is an infringement of copyright.
Infringers are liable under the law.

Visit Hal Leonard Online at
www.halleonard.com

Hi! My name is Charlie Brown, and this is the Peanuts™ Music Activity Book. We're going to have lots of fun together. We'll learn about music and play and sing some of my favorite Peanuts™ songs. If you've seen us on TV or at the movies, many of these songs will be familiar to you. In addition to the songs there are plenty of games, puzzles, and other activities for you to enjoy.

If this is the first time you've ever learned about music, that's okay! We'll start at the beginning. Linus, Lucy, Sally, Schroeder, and the rest of the gang will be here to help. You can also ask a grownup to join you in the fun.

Speaking of fun, let's get started!

Contents

Notes 4	Baseball Theme 40
The Music Alphabet 5	More About Sharps and Flats 42
Long and Short Notes 6	Music Math 43
Your First Song 6	Eighth Notes 44
Mary Had a Little Lamb 7	Counting Eighth Notes 45
The Staff 8	Fermata 47
Notes on the Staff 9	Happy Birthday to You 47
The Keyboard 10	Eighth Rests 48
Name the Keys 11	Rhythm Word Search 49
Play and Sing the Music Alphabet 12	Time for a Rest 49
Charlie Brown Theme 12	Happiness Theme 50
Yankee Doodle 13	Red Baron 52
Note Values 14	Heart and Soul 54
Coloring Fun 15	This Land Is Your Land 56
Connect the Dots 16	Dotted Notes 58
How Music Is Organized 17	Note Matching 59
Counting Notes in 3/4 Time 18	Christmas Time Is Here 60
Take Me Out to the Ball Game 18	Maze Fun 62
Counting Notes in 4/4 Time 20	O Tannenbaum 63
Twinkle, Twinkle Little Star 20	Linus and Lucy 66
Add the Missing Bar Lines 22	Triplets 68
Ode to Joy 22	Charlie Brown Theme 70
Rests 24	The Great Pumpkin Waltz 72
Bingo 24	Triplet Fun 75
Crossword Fun 26	Schroeder 76
Note Reading Review 27	Für Elise 78
Pick-up Notes 28	Syncopation 80
Oh Where, Oh Where Has My Little Dog Gone? 28	Joe Cool 81
Repeat Sign 29	Word Search 82
Steps and Skips 30	D.C. al Coda 83
Sharps 32	Dynamics 83
Sharps in Space 33	Skating 84
Hark, the Herald Angels Sing 34	Hound Dog 88
Flats 36	He's Your Dog, Charlie Brown 91
Rain, Rain, Go Away 37	Peppermint Patty 92
Sharp or Flat? 38	Chopsticks (solo) 94
Ties 39	Chopsticks (duet) 95
1st and 2nd Endings 39	Answer Key 96

Notes

When people sing or play a musical instrument, the sound they make can be written down with musical symbols called *notes*. The notes can be put together, one by one, to make a big piece of music, like a song.

Imagine that each note is a bead. The same way you can put beads together to make a beautiful necklace, you can put notes together to make music.

Some notes sound *high*; some notes sound *low*.

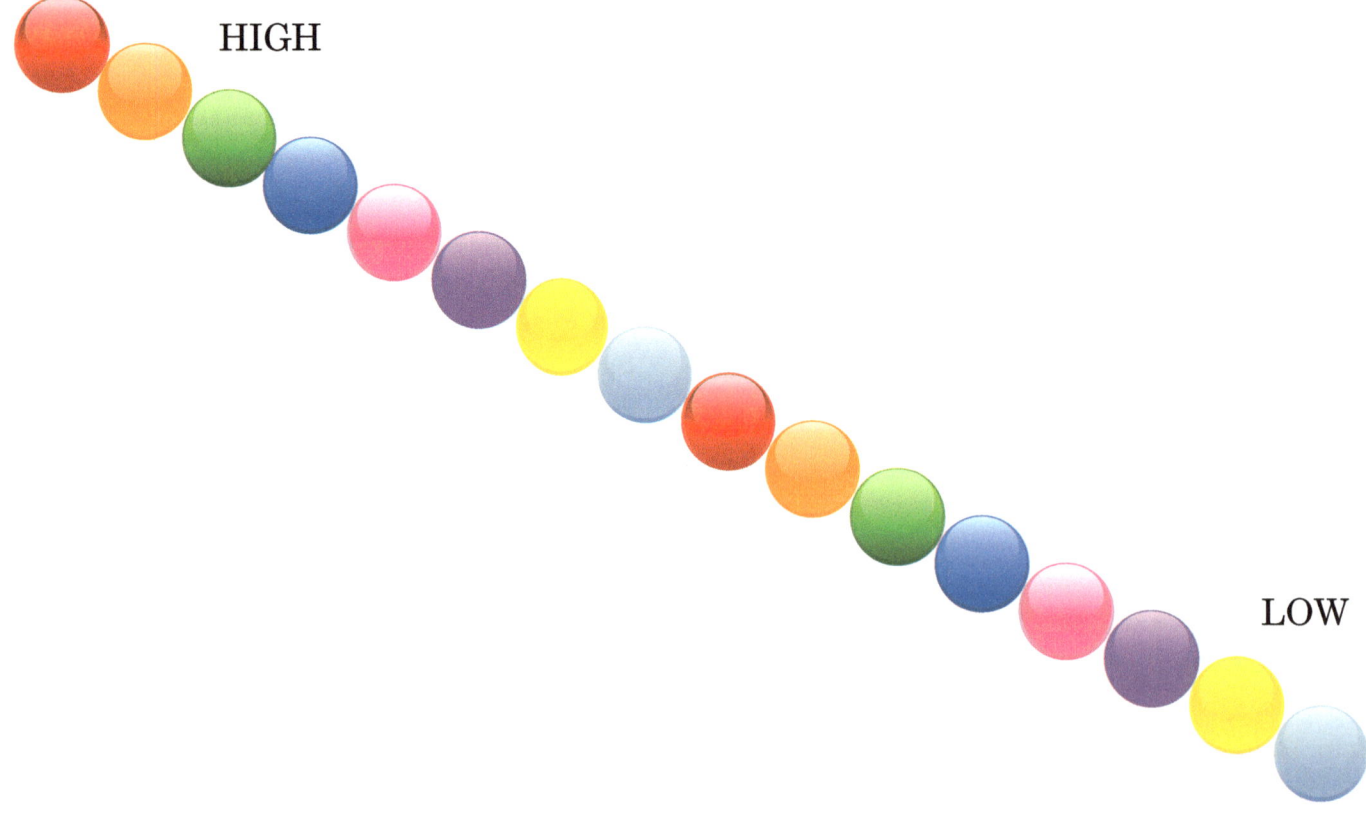

The Music Alphabet

Different notes have different names.
But they don't have names like "Charlie,"
or "Lucy." Notes have letter names.
The Music Alphabet is easy because it uses
only seven letters: A, B, C, D, E, F, and G.

Notes on paper are round. In this book, the letter name of each note is written in the middle of the circle. And to help you while you are first learning the note names, each note has its own color:

The Music Alphabet uses the same seven letters over and over again, from low to high, and backwards, from high to low.

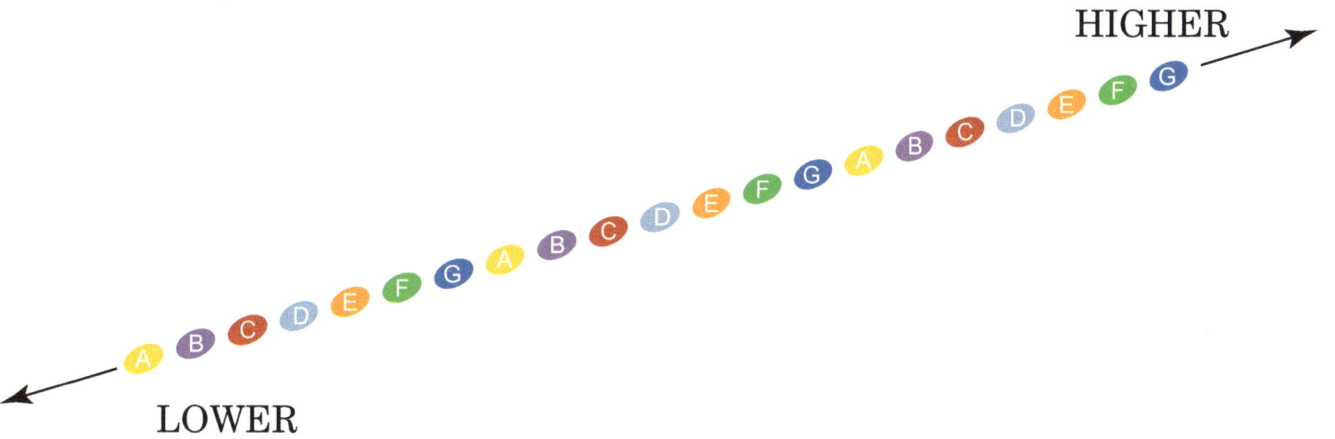

HIGHER

LOWER

Long and Short Notes

You already know that some notes sound high and some notes sound low. You also know that different notes have different letter names.

But maybe you didn't know that some notes sound long, and some notes sound short. Take a look at "Mary Had a Little Lamb" on the next page. Sing the first line: "Mary had a little lamb." When you sing the word "lamb" you hold it for a longer time than the words that came before it. "Lamb" has a note that is long. The notes before "lamb" are shorter.

Long notes are white Ⓔ ; short notes are black ●.
You can also tell how long a note is by looking at the colored bar above the note. The longer the colored bar, the longer the note.

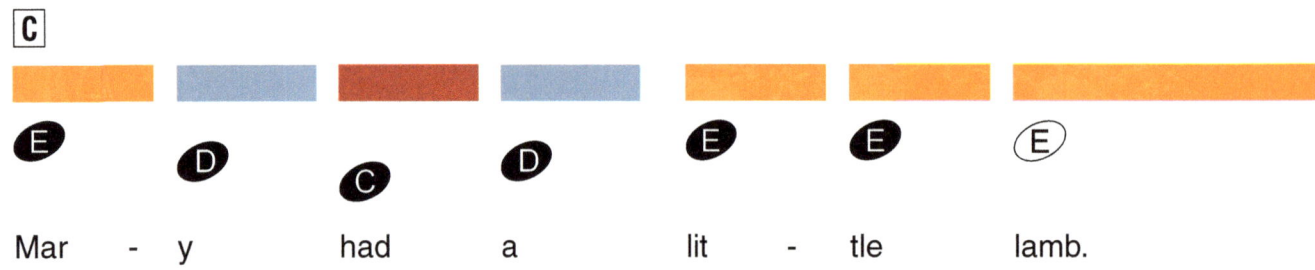

Your First Song

"Mary Had a Little Lamb" is the first song in this book. Try singing it, and ask a grownup to help you if you need help.

If you look closely at the song, you'll see something that we haven't talked about yet. There are letters in boxes above the colored bars, like this: C, G. These are called *chord symbols*, and they are in the music for someone to play along with you on a guitar or a keyboard. If you know someone who can play along, the chord symbols are the part they should play. But even without the chords, you can still play and sing the songs!

Mary Had a Little Lamb

Words by Sarah Josepha Hale
Traditional Music

C						
E	D	C	D	E	E	E
Mar-	y	had	a	lit-	tle	lamb,

G			C		
D	D	D	E	G	G
lit-	tle	lamb,	lit-	tle	lamb.

E	D	C	D	E	E	E	E
Mar-	y	had	a	lit-	tle	lamb	whose

G				C		
D	D	E	D	C		
fleece	was	white	as	snow.		

Copyright © 2015 by HAL LEONARD CORPORATION
International Copyright Secured   All Rights Reserved

The Staff

To make it easier to see which notes are higher or lower than others, music notes are written on a set of five lines and four spaces called a *staff*. At the beginning of the staff is a *clef sign* to name the lines and spaces. The clef sign we will use is called the *Treble Clef*.

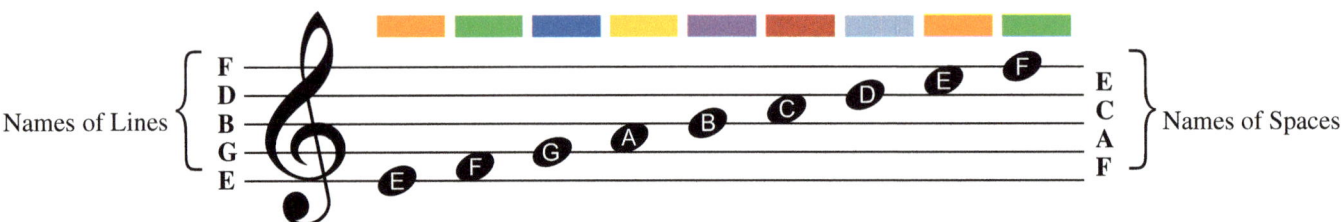

As you can see, each line and space on the staff has a letter name of its own. Each note on a particular line or in a particular space has the same name.

It's easy to remember the names of the lines and spaces. From bottom to the top the *lines* are: **E-G-B-D-F**. One way to remember this is to say, "**E**very **G**ood **B**oy **D**oes **F**ine."

From bottom to top the *spaces* are named **F-A-C-E**. This is easy to remember because the names of the spaces spell "face."

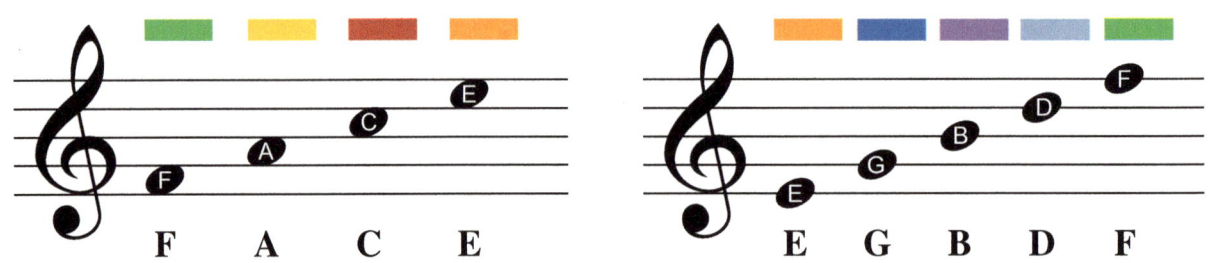

If a note is too high or too low to fit on the staff, extra lines can be added. These short lines are called *ledger lines*.

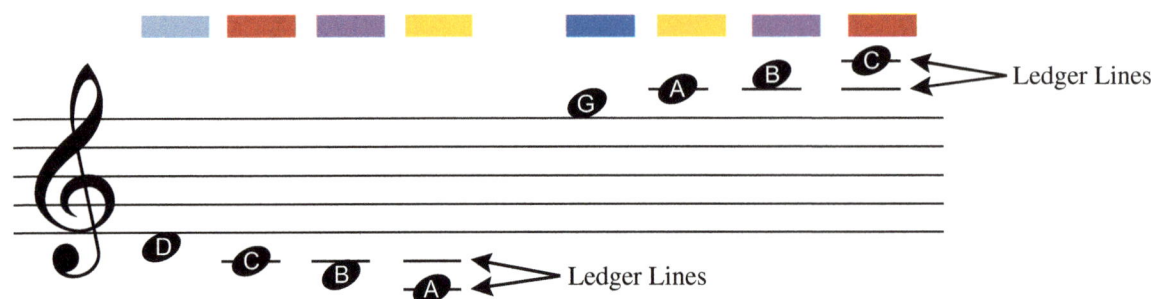

Notes on the Staff

These notes on the staff spell words. Place the notes on the correct line or space. The first one is done for you.

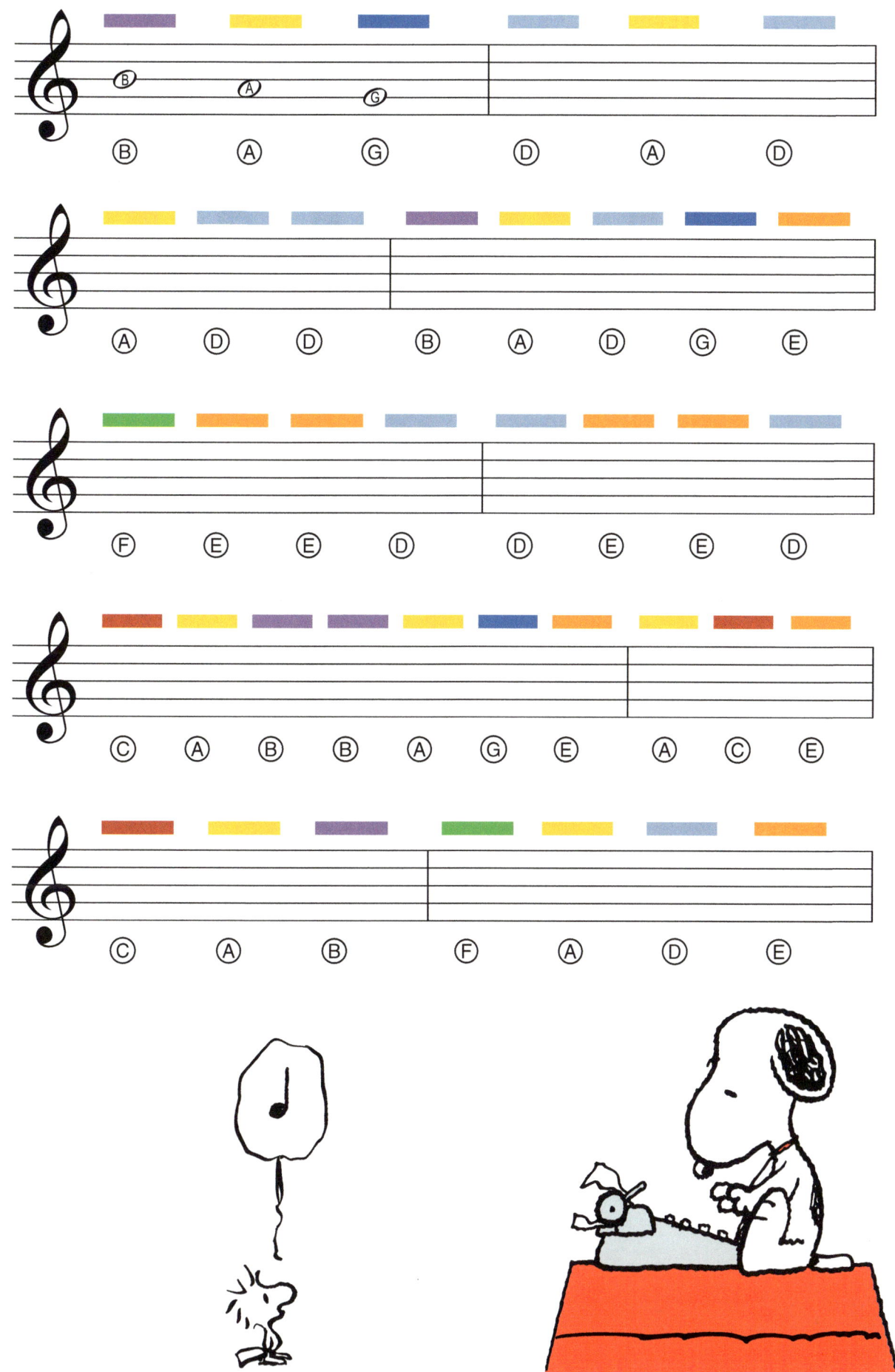

The Keyboard

It's easy to play notes on the piano keyboard. The keyboard is organized in groups of *black keys* and *white keys*. Take a look at the keyboard below to see the pattern of black key groups.

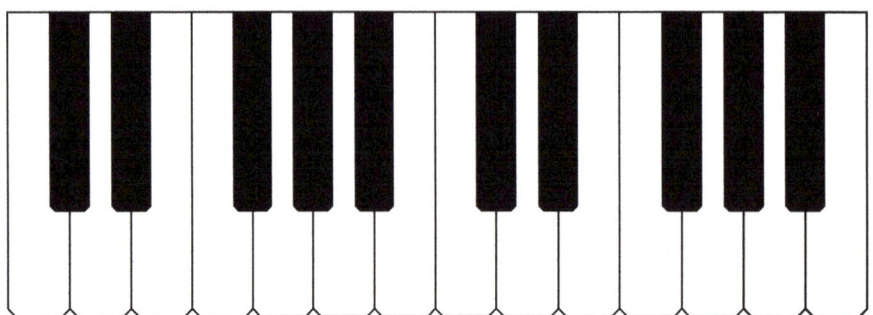

The white keys are named just like the notes on the staff, using the seven letters of the music alphabet.

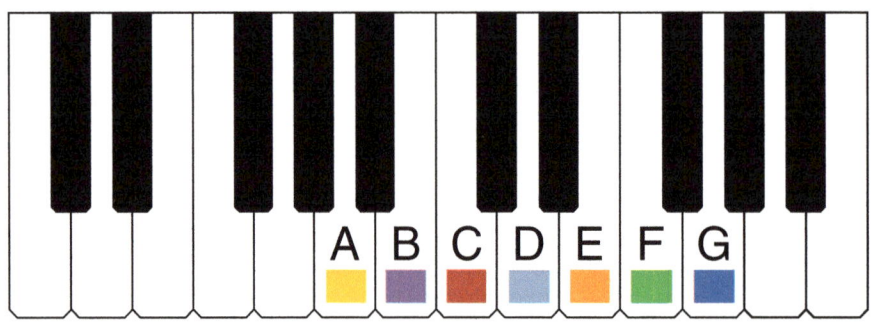

To help you learn the names of the white keys, we've included colored stickers for you to place on your keyboard. Carefully attach them using the directions found on the sticker sheet.

Finger numbers tell us which finger to use when we play notes on the keyboard. We number the fingers 1-5, and thumb is always number 1.

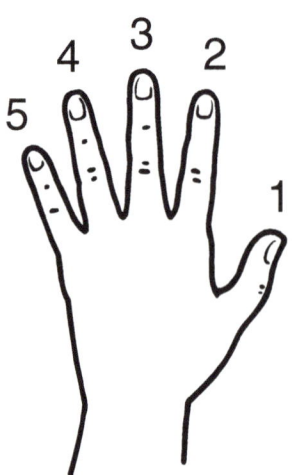
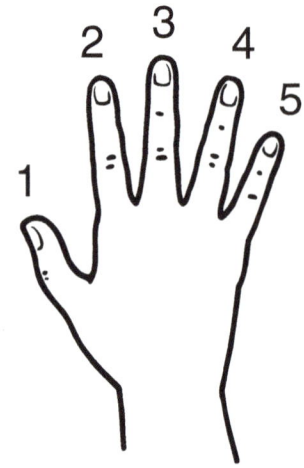

Left Hand (L.H.) Right Hand (R.H.)

Name the Keys

Practice naming the white keys on the keyboards below.

Color all the Cs, Ds, and Es. These notes touch the groups of two black keys.

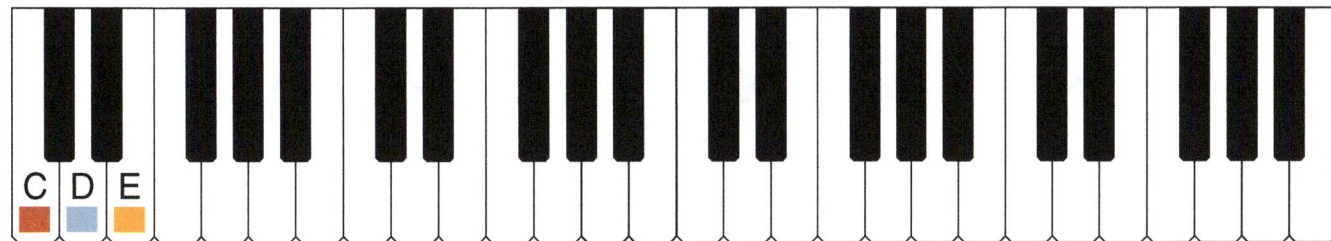

Color all the Fs, Gs, As, and Bs. These notes touch the groups of three black keys.

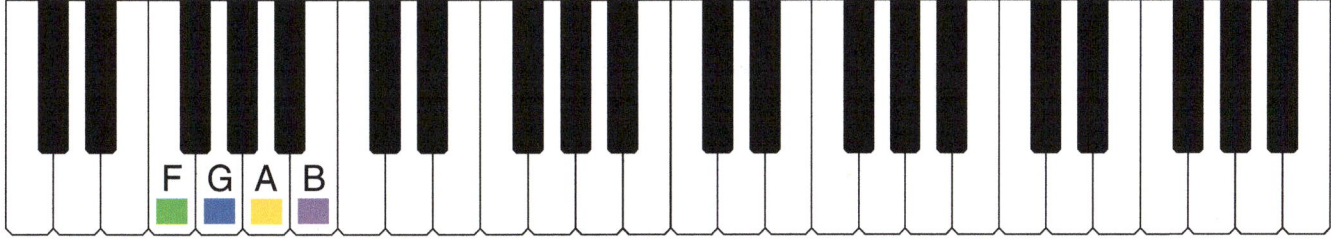

Fill in the names of the missing keys:

Use the finger numbers given to play white keys on your keyboard.

Use your right hand to play all the Cs on your keyboard with finger 2.
Use your left hand to play all the Gs on your keyboard with finger 3.
Use your right hand to play all the As with finger 4.
Use your right hand to play all the Ds with finger 3.
Use your left hand to play all the Es with finger 2.
Use your right hand to play the highest B with finger 5.
Use your left hand to play the lowest F with finger 1.

Play and Sing the Music Alphabet

Here are two songs to help you play and sing the music alphabet.
Learn them well so we can dance to them! Sing the note names as you play.

CHARLIE BROWN THEME

The small keyboard shows you which fingers you will use.

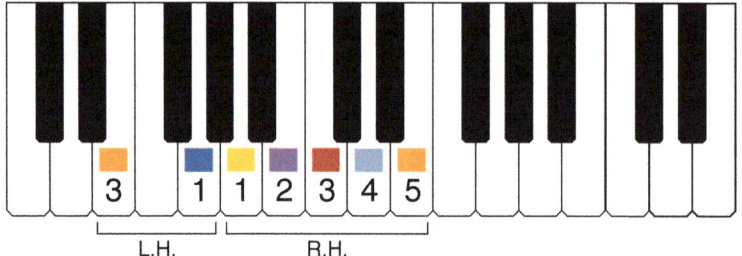

By Vince Guaraldi

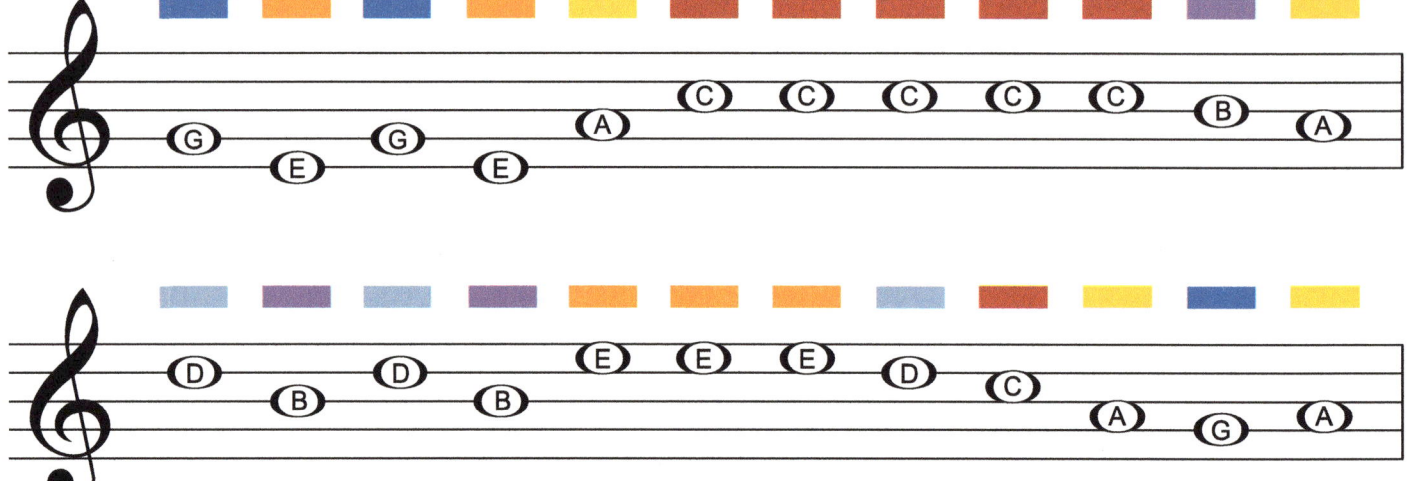

Copyright © 1964 LEE MENDELSON FILM PRODUCTIONS, INC.
Copyright Renewed
International Copyright Secured   All Rights Reserved

YANKEE DOODLE

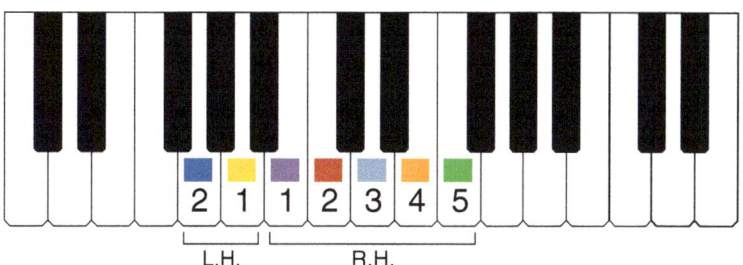

Traditional

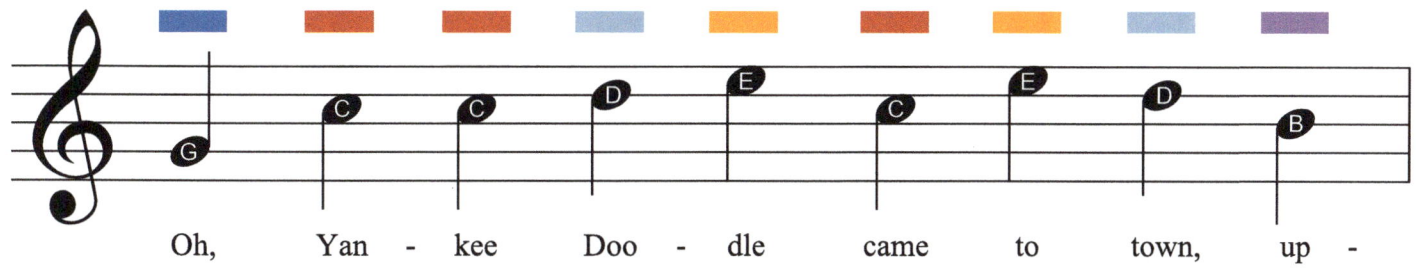

Oh, Yan - kee Doo - dle came to town, up -

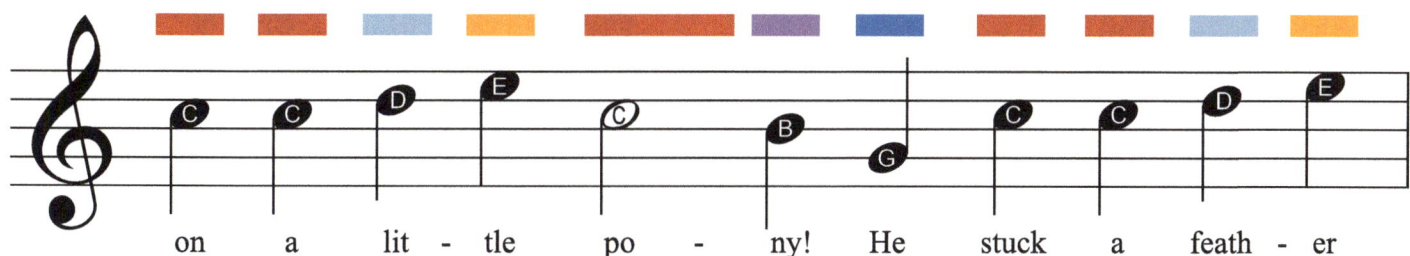

on a lit - tle po - ny! He stuck a feath - er

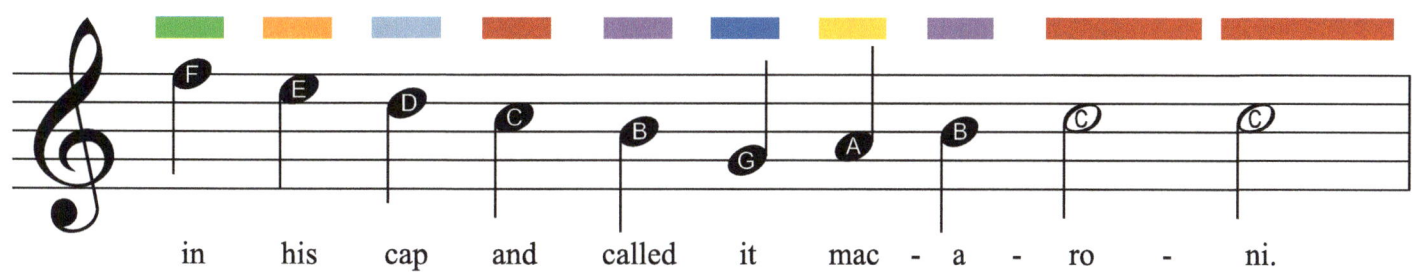

in his cap and called it mac - a - ro - ni.

Copyright © 2015 by HAL LEONARD CORPORATION
International Copyright Secured   All Rights Reserved

Note Values

A music note tells us two things: how high or low a sound is, and how long the sound lasts.

You already know how high or low a note will sound by where it is on the staff. You also know that black notes are short, and white notes are long. But that isn't enough. We need to be more exact about how long the notes are.

Note values are measured in *beats*. When you tap your foot or clap your hands along with a song, you are tapping or clapping the *beat*.

The longest note value in most music is a *whole note*. The chart below shows how a whole note (and a pizza!) can be divided into smaller pieces of equal size.

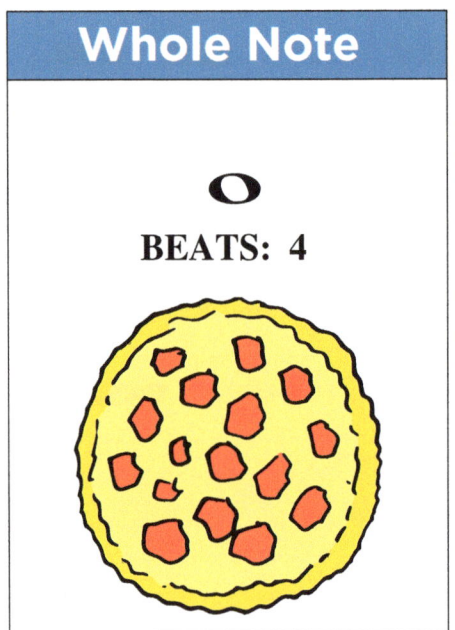

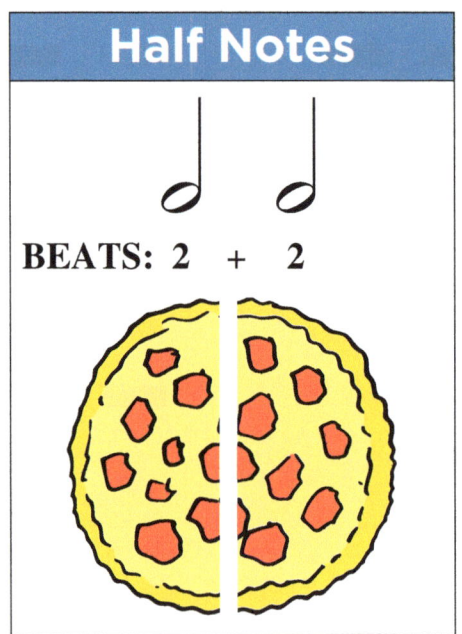

Coloring Fun

Use the note values to color Charlie Brown.
If the note equals 4 beats, color those areas yellow.
If the note equals 2 beats, color those areas blue.
If the note equals 1 beat, color those areas brown.

Connect the Dots

Can you name this symbol?

What makes music fun is the way the seven letters
of the music alphabet and the long and short notes
get all mixed up together to make songs.

How Music Is Organized

You already know about the *staff*, which shows you how high or low the notes are. Here's the staff with some added music symbols to help you read the notes. You'll always find a *clef sign* at the beginning of the song. *Bar lines* divide the staff into *measures*, which contain groups of beats. Right next to the clef sign is a *time signature*. The top number tells you how many beats are in each measure. The 4 on the bottom reminds you that a quarter note equals one beat. There is a *double bar line* at the end of the staff. This sign tells you where the song ends.

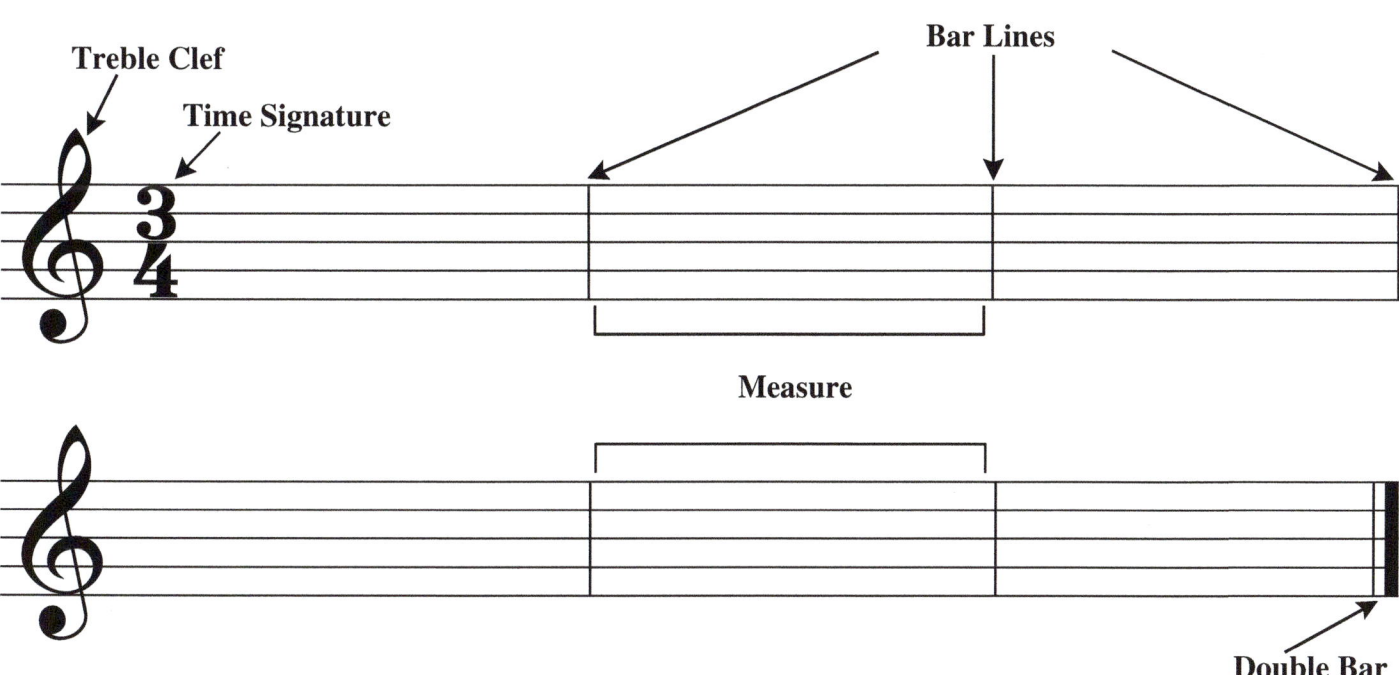

Counting Notes in 3/4 Time

Here's a new note, the dotted half note: 𝅗𝅥.

A dotted half note looks like a half note with an added dot. This note equals three beats.

"Take Me Out to the Ball Game" has a 3/4 time signature. The number 3 on top tells us there are three beats in each measure. Tap your foot or count along with the numbers "1-2-3" for each measure to make sure that you keep a steady beat.

TAKE ME OUT TO THE BALL GAME

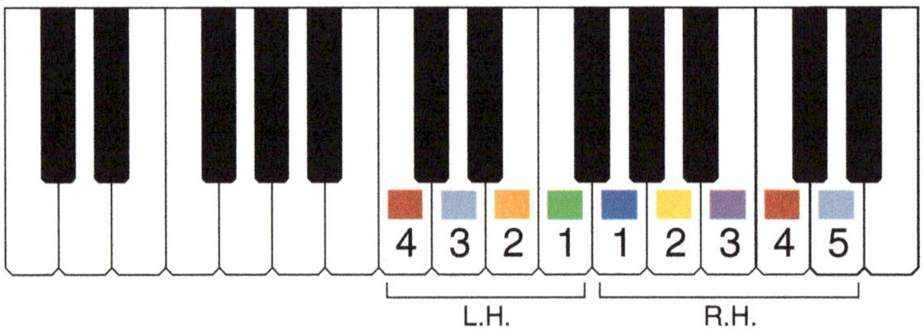

Words by Jack Norworth
Music by Albert von Tilzer

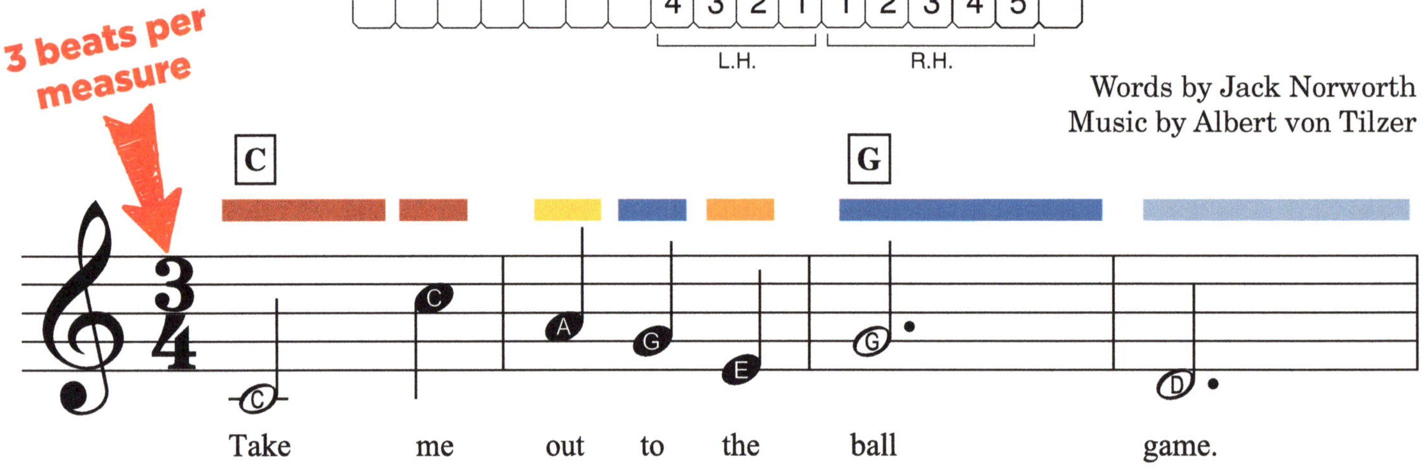

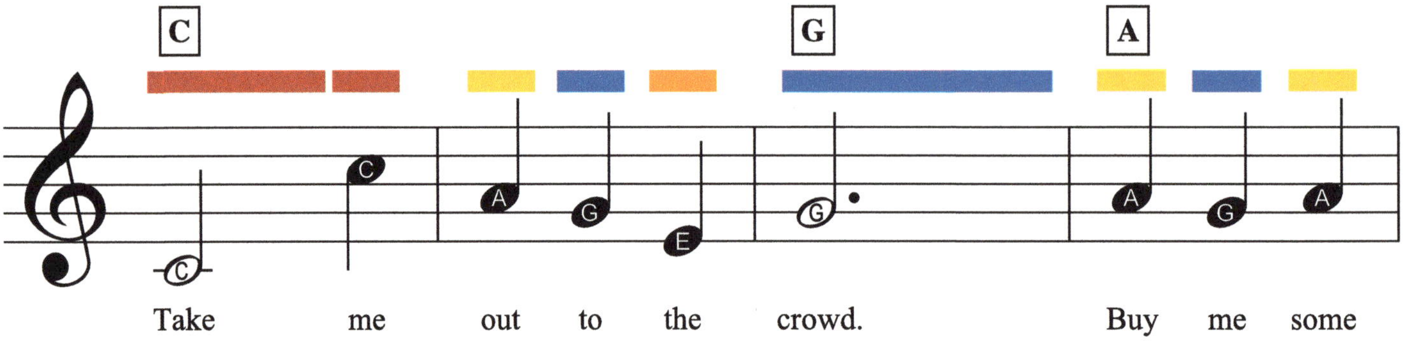

3 beats per measure

Take me out to the ball game.
Take me out to the crowd. Buy me some

Copyright © 2015 by HAL LEONARD CORPORATION
International Copyright Secured   All Rights Reserved

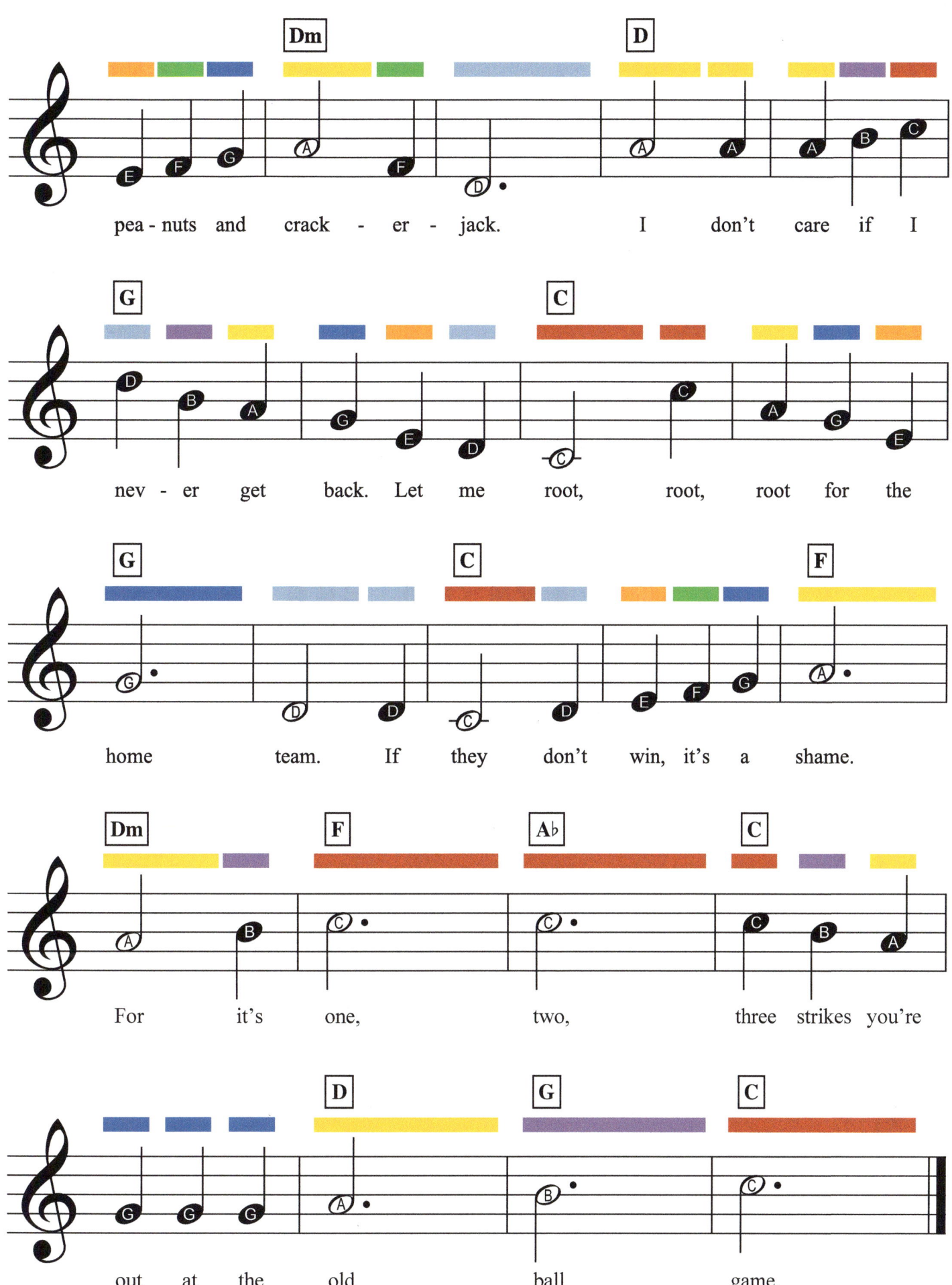

Counting Notes in 4/4 Time

"Twinkle, Twinkle Little Star" has a 4/4 time signature. The number 4 on top tells us there are four beats in each measure. Tap or count along to make sure you keep four steady beats in each measure.

TWINKLE, TWINKLE LITTLE STAR

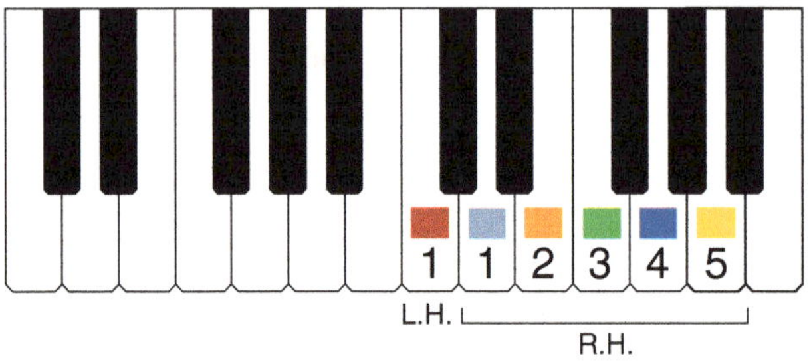

Traditional

4 beats per measure

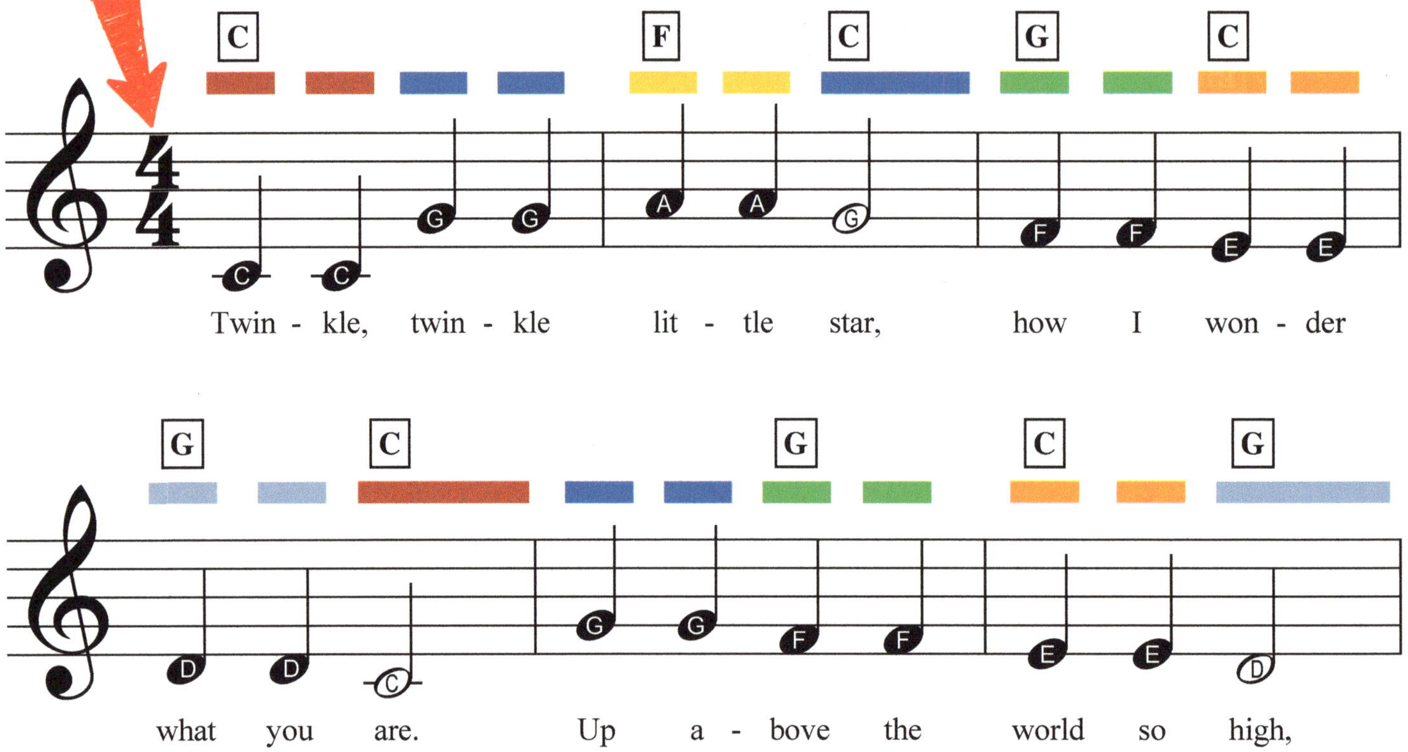

Twin - kle, twin - kle lit - tle star, how I won - der what you are. Up a - bove the world so high,

Copyright © 2015 by HAL LEONARD CORPORATION
International Copyright Secured   All Rights Reserved

Add the Missing Bar Lines

You know that bar lines divide music into measures. And you know that the time signature tells us how many beats are in each measure. Our next song has four beats in each measure. Draw the bar lines where they are needed before you play "Ode to Joy." To check whether you've put the bar lines in the right places, see page 96.

By Ludwig van Beethoven

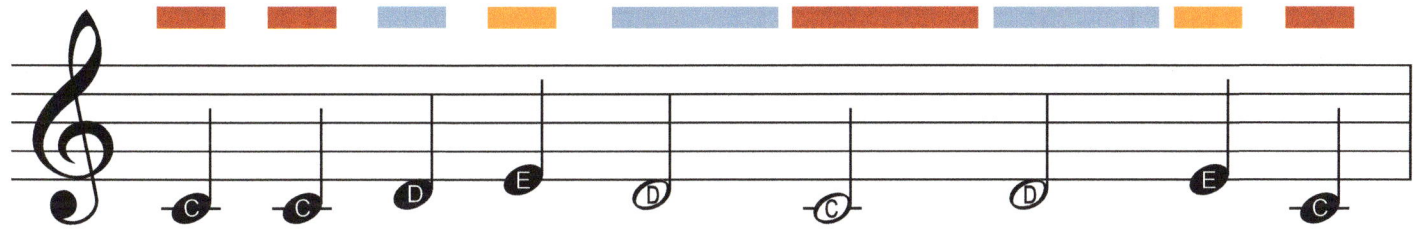
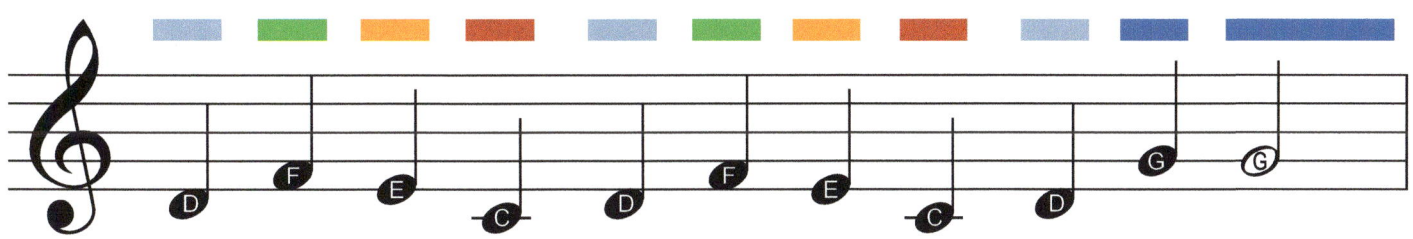
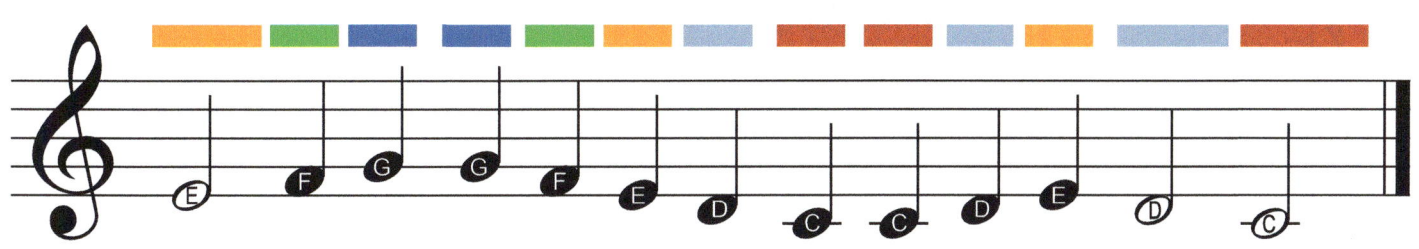

Rests

Rests are music symbols that stand for silence. A rest will tell you when **not** to play a note. Like notes, each rest is worth a certain number of beats, as shown below.

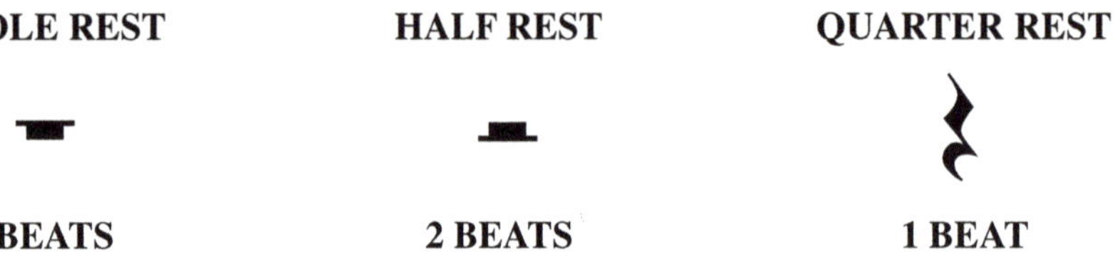

WHOLE REST	HALF REST	QUARTER REST
4 BEATS	2 BEATS	1 BEAT

Quarter rests and a half rest appear in our next song, "Bingo" When you come to the rest, count the beats until it's time to play the next melody note. Practice counting rests in the examples below.

1. [musical notation: 4/4 time, half rest, quarter rest, G quarter note | C C C G — "There was a far-mer" counted (1 2 3) 4 | 1 2 3 4]

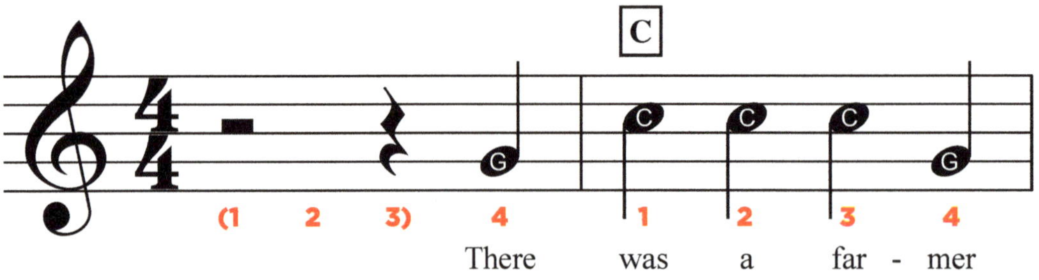

2. [musical notation: 4/4 time, E E E E | quarter rest F F F — "B-I-N-G-O." counted 1 2 3 4 | (1) 2 3 4]

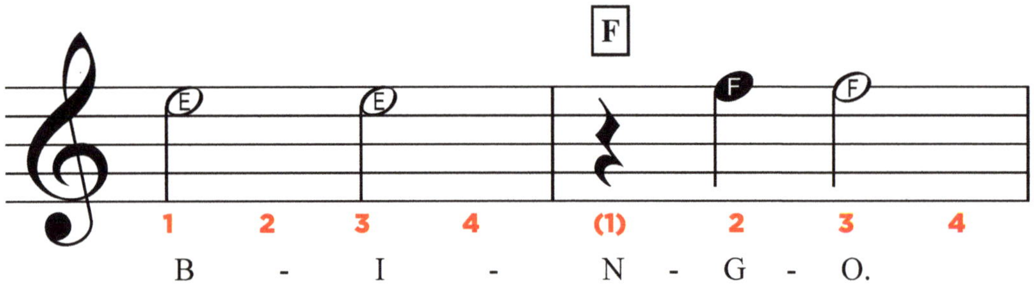

BINGO

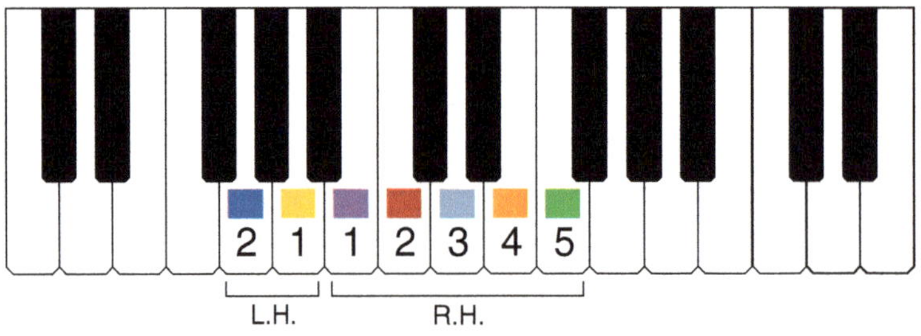

Traditional

[keyboard diagram with colored keys labeled L.H. 2 1 and R.H. 1 2 3 4 5]

[musical notation: 4/4 time, half rest, quarter rest, G | C C C G | A A G G — "There was a far-mer had a dog and"]

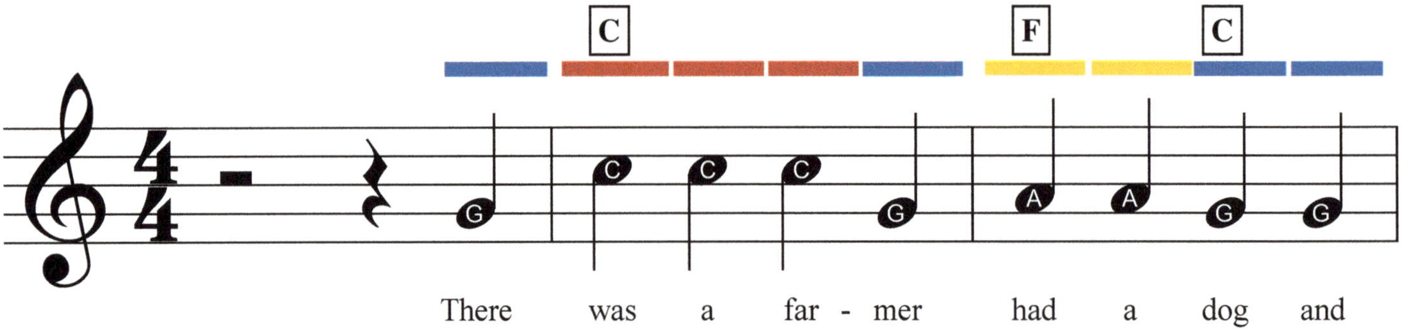

Copyright © 2015 by HAL LEONARD CORPORATION
International Copyright Secured   All Rights Reserved

Crossword Fun

ACROSS

1. The top number of a time signature tells you how many _____ are in a measure.
5. Notes that are too high or too low to fit on the staff are written using ledger _____.
7. White notes are long. Black notes are _____.
11. A double _____ tells you where the song ends.
13. A _____ is the space between two bar lines.
14. The letter names of the spaces on the staff, from bottom to top, spell this word.
15. A treble _____ appears at the beginning of a song.
16. The bottom number of a time signature tells you what kind of note is one _____ long.
17. The same way you can put beads together to make a necklace, you can put _____ together to make music.
18. A whole note lasts _____ beats.
19. Black notes are short. White notes are _____.

DOWN

2. In $\frac{3}{4}$ time there are _____ beats in every measure.
3. You can divide a whole note into smaller pieces, just like a _____.
4. The _____ half note lasts for three beats.
6. Notes are written on the _____, which has five lines.
8. A _____ note lasts two beats.
9. In $\frac{4}{4}$ time the _____ note is one beat long.
10. There are _____ letters in the music alphabet.
12. The letters in the music alphabet are:

Answers on page 96.

Note Reading Review

Name the notes and color Charlie Brown and his friends with crayons, pencils or markers using the note and color key at the bottom of the page.

orange   pink   brown   yellow   red   light blue

Pick-up Notes

Your next song, "Oh Where, Oh Where Has My Little Dog Gone?" starts with a *pick-up note*, a melody note played before the first full measure. This pick-up note is a quarter note, or one beat. You may wonder where the other two beats in the measure are. Take a look at the end of the song. As you know, two quarter rests are worth two beats. These two quarter rests plus the quarter note pick-up equal three beats—one full measure.

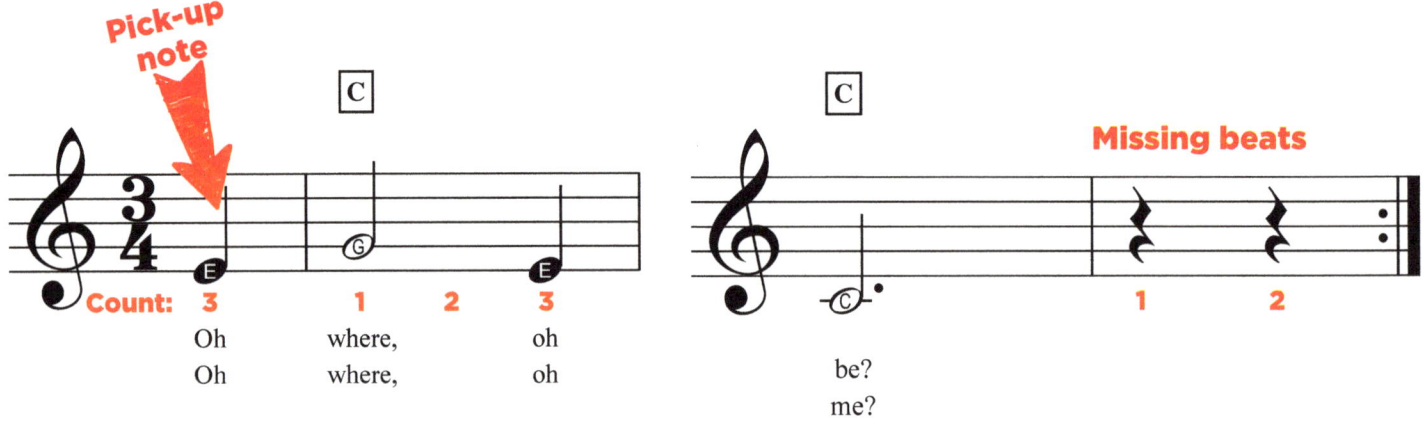

OH WHERE, OH WHERE HAS MY LITTLE DOG GONE?

Words by Sep. Winner
Traditional Melody

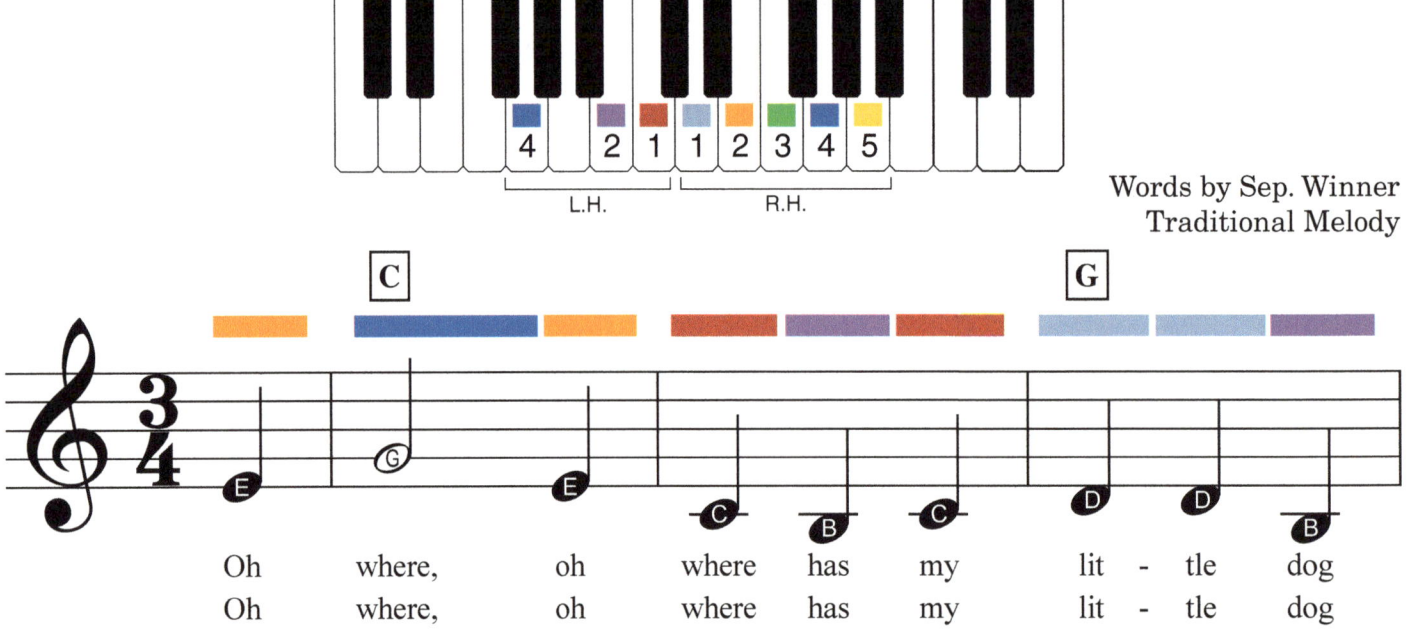

Copyright © 2015 by HAL LEONARD CORPORATION
International Copyright Secured   All Rights Reserved

(Sheet music: "Oh Where, Oh Where Has My Little Dog Gone?")

Verse 1: gone? Oh where, oh where can he be? With his hair so short and his tail so long, oh where, oh where can he be?

Verse 2: gone? Oh where, oh where can he be? If you see him an-y-where, won't you please bring back my dog-gie to me?

Repeat Sign

A *Repeat Sign* is used at the end of "Oh Where, Oh Where Has My Little Dog Gone?" This music symbol tells you to go back to the beginning of the song and play it again. When this happens, there is usually more than one set of words (*verses*) below the melody notes.

29

Steps and Skips

When notes on the staff move from a space to a line, or a line to a space, we can describe that distance as a *step*.

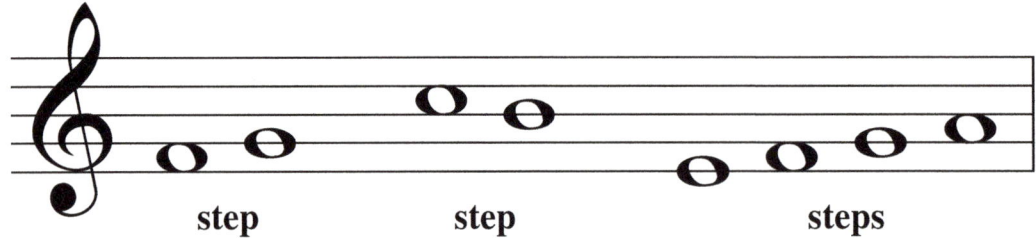

On the keyboard, a step is the distance from one key to the very next key. Steps can move up or down.

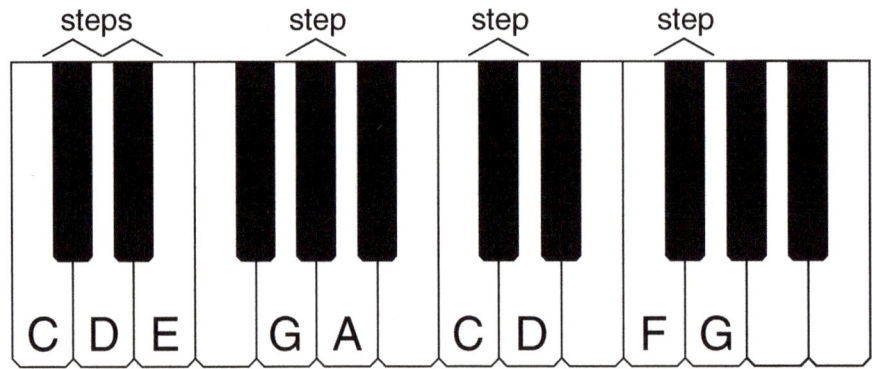

When notes are written from one line to the next line, or from a space to the next space, we call that distance a *skip*.

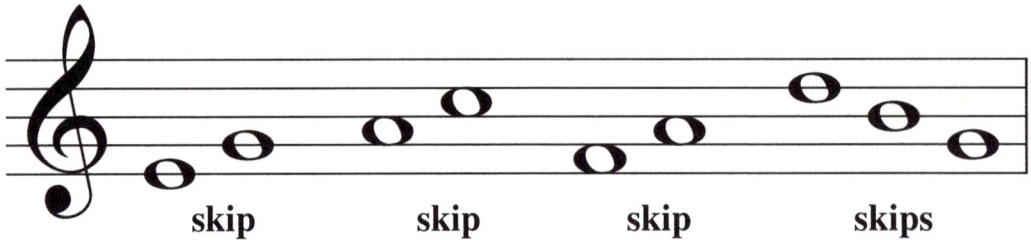

On the keyboard, we skip a white key when we skip a line or space on the staff. We can skip up or down.

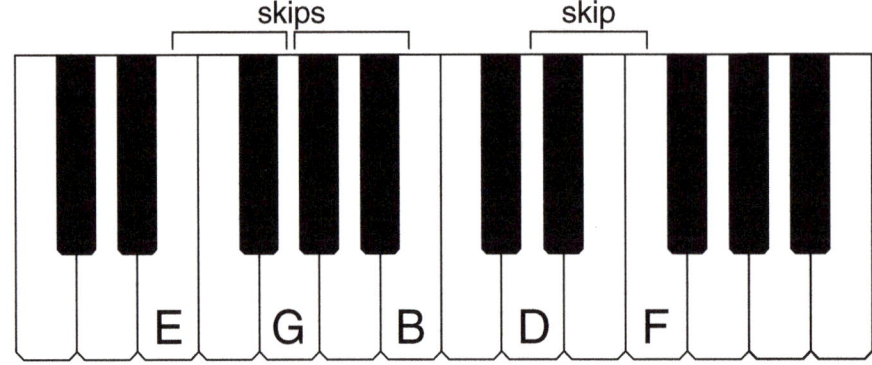

On the keyboards below, write in the note names to show steps or skips.

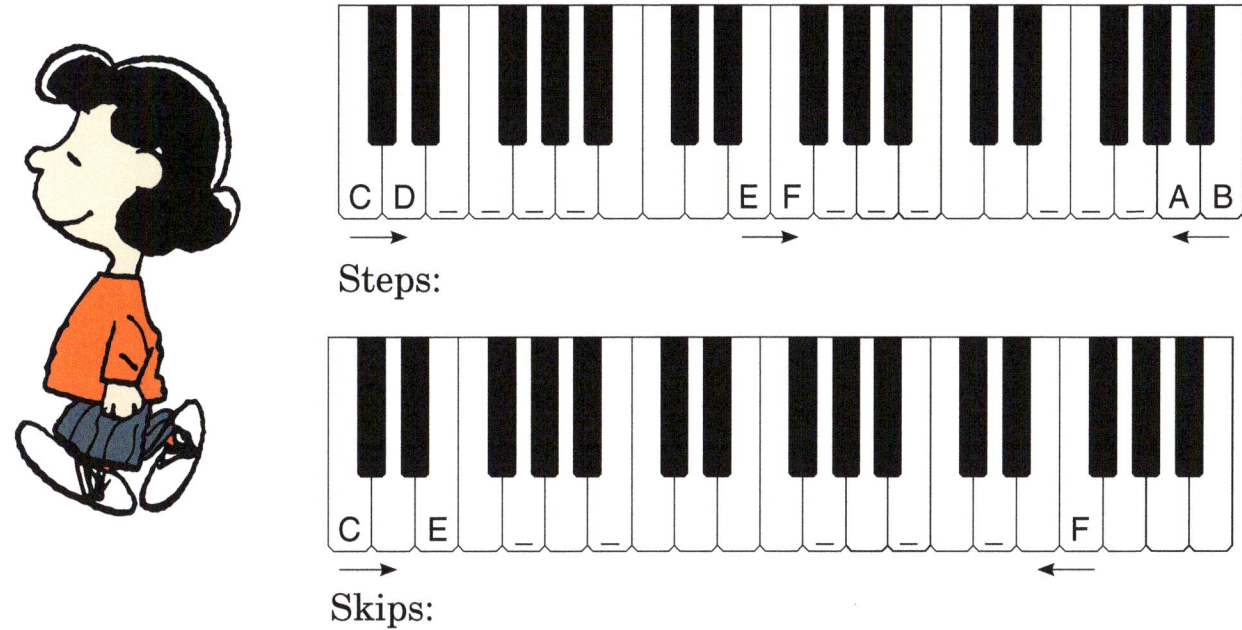

Steps:

Skips:

On the staff below, label the notes as steps or skips.
The first example is done for you.

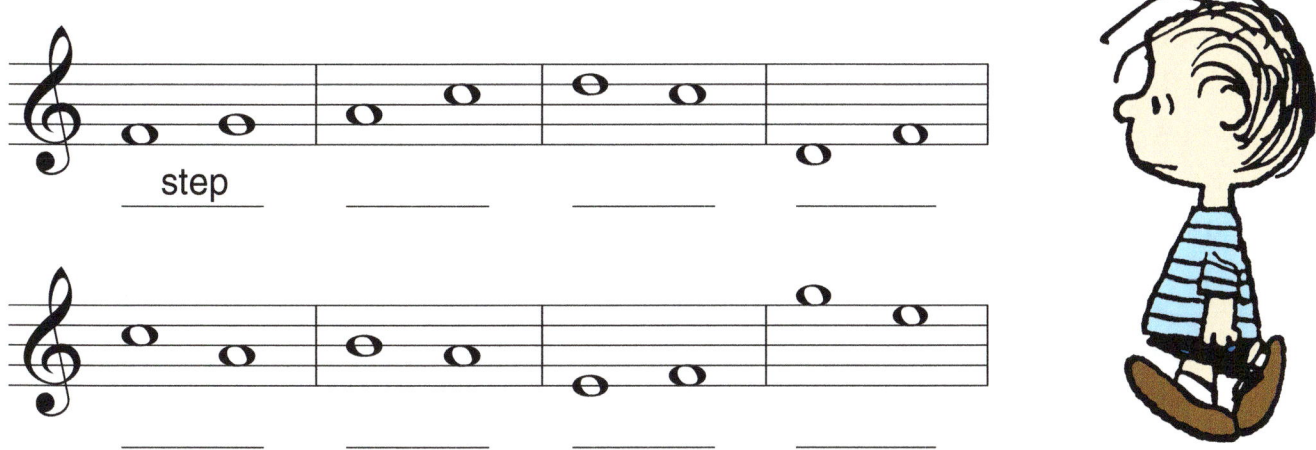

step

In each measure below, draw notes that step or skip.

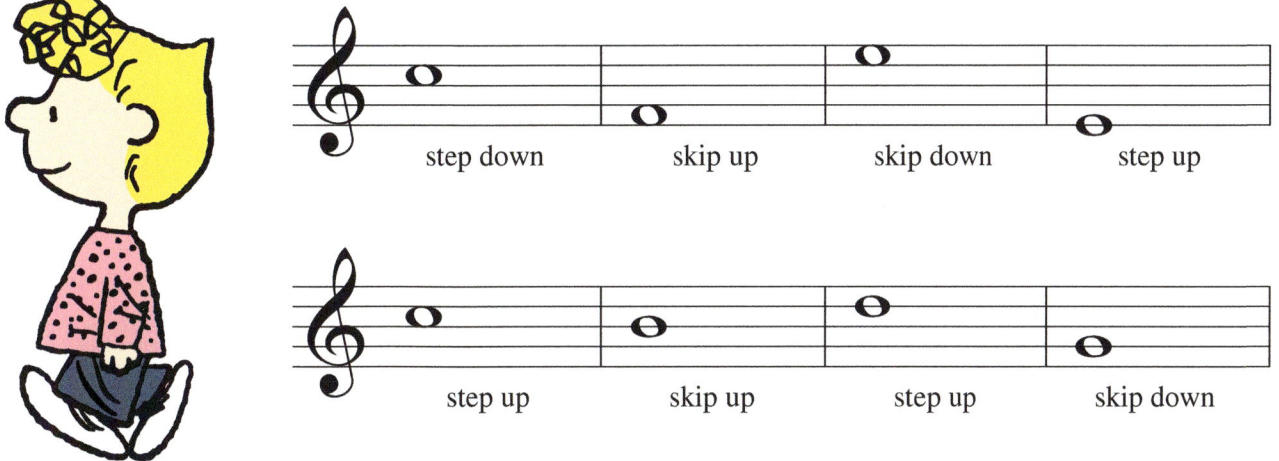

step down   skip up   skip down   step up

step up   skip up   step up   skip down

Answers on page 96.

Sharps

You know the seven letters of the music alphabet pretty well by now. You're ready to learn some new notes. One way to show some of these notes is with a *sharp sign*, which looks like this: ♯

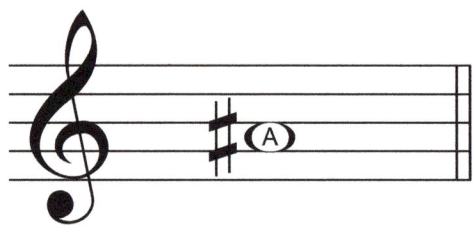

The name of this note is not A anymore—it's *A sharp* (A♯).

A note with a sharp in front of it sounds a half step higher than it would without the sharp. A *half step* is a very small distance in music. On a keyboard, we describe it as one key to the **very next** key—often a white key to black key.

Sharped notes are usually between two musical letter names. For example, A♯ is between A and B. This is easiest to see on the keyboard, where sharped notes are usually black keys.

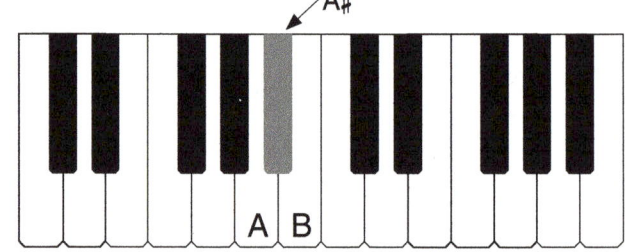

REMEMBER, WHEN YOU SEE A SHARP IN FRONT OF A NOTE, PLAY OR SING A HALF STEP HIGHER. A NOTE WITH A SHARP SOUNDS A LITTLE HIGHER THAN THE SAME NOTE WITHOUT A SHARP.

Sharps in Space

Draw a line connecting the sharped notes on the staff to the notes on the keyboards below. Check your answers on page 96.

33

There is one sharped note in "Hark, the Herald Angels Sing." Can you find it? Play the F♯ first with your left hand, and in the very last measure, play it with your right hand finger 4 as marked for you on the small keyboard above the song.

HARK, THE HERALD ANGELS SING

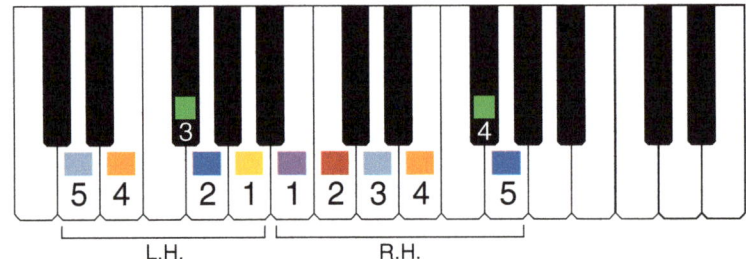

from A CHARLIE BROWN CHRISTMAS
Traditional
Arranged by Vince Guaraldi

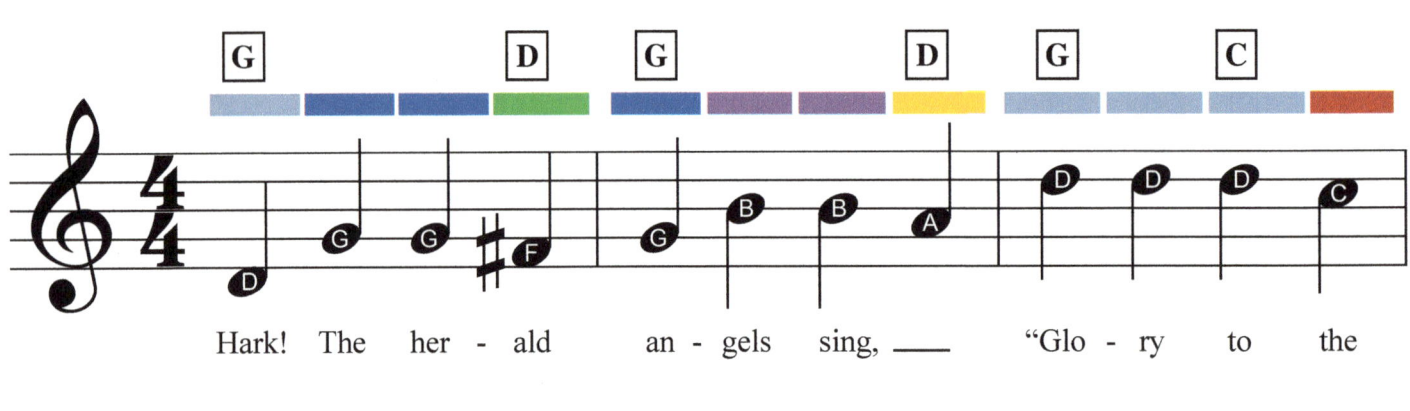

Hark! The her - ald an - gels sing, ___ "Glo - ry to the

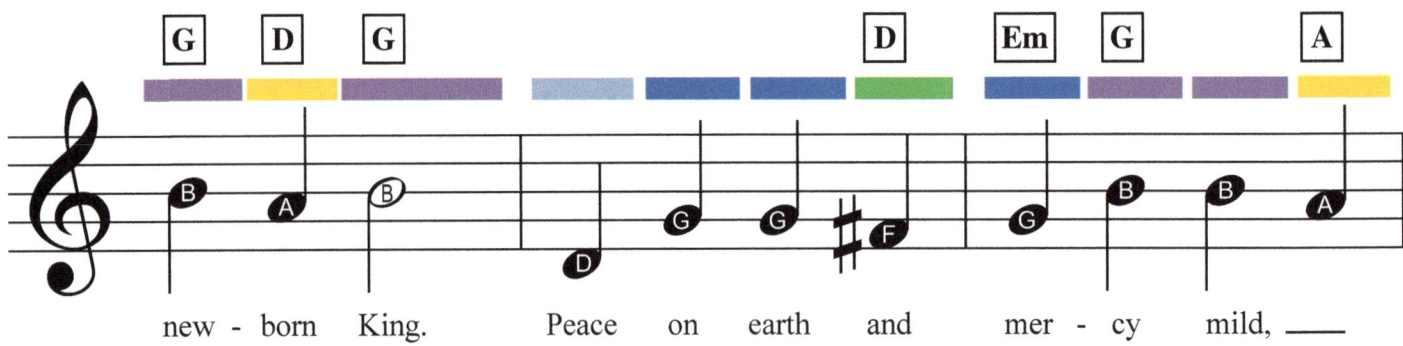

new - born King. Peace on earth and mer - cy mild, ___

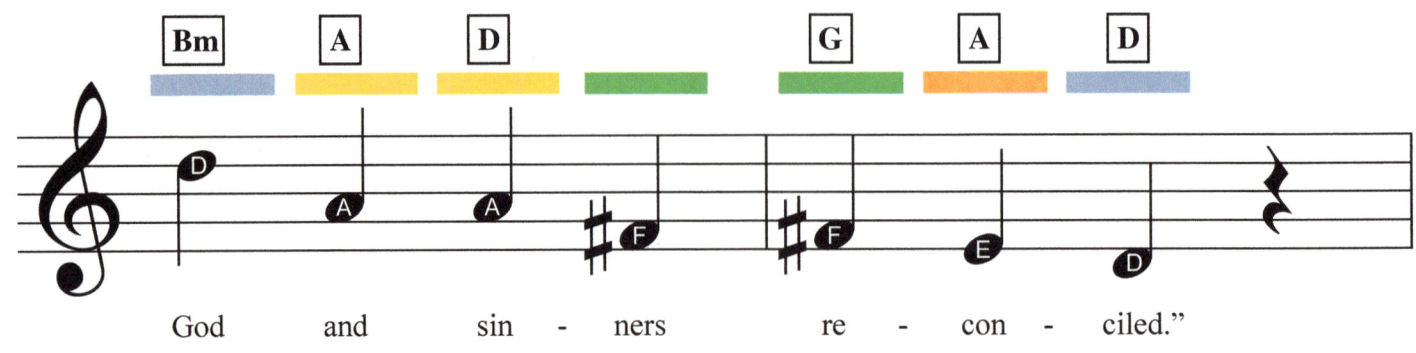

God and sin - ners re - con - ciled."

Copyright © 1965 LEE MENDELSON FILM PRODUCTIONS, INC.
Copyright Renewed
International Copyright Secured   All Rights Reserved

Flats

In our next song, "Rain, Rain, Go Away," you'll see a note with a flat in front of it, like this:

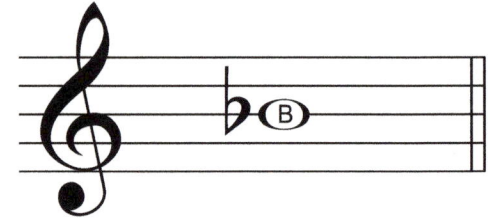

A note with a flat in front of it is a half step *lower* than it would be without the flat.

The flat is added to the name of the note. In this example, the name of the note is not B anymore, it's **B-flat**, also written: **B♭**

Just like sharps, flat notes usually fall between two letter name notes. For example, B♭ is between A and B. On keyboard instruments, flat notes are usually black keys.

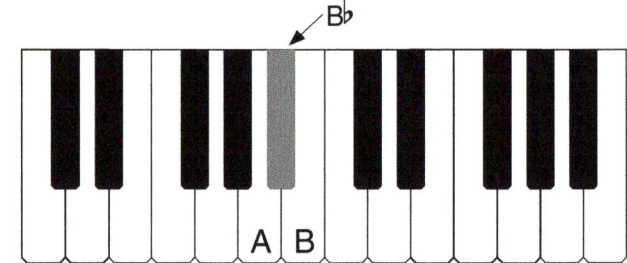

> WAIT A MINUTE! BEFORE YOU SAID THAT A♯ IS BETWEEN A AND B. NOW YOU'RE SAYING THAT B♭ IS BETWEEN A AND B! ARE YOU TRYING TO GET ME MIXED UP?

No, we're not trying to get Marcie mixed up. That black key between A and B can be called either sharp or flat. Check out the keyboard below. The black keys get their name from the white keys. When going *up* the scale, the black keys have "sharp" names. When going *down* the scale, the black keys have "flat" names.

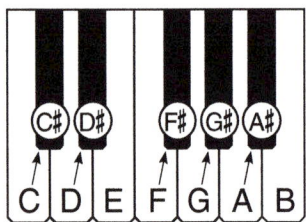 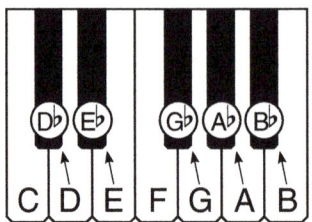

Just remember, when you see a **flat** in front of a note, play the very next note **lower** on the keyboard. When you see a **sharp** in front of a note, play the very next note **higher** on the keyboard.

By Vince Guaraldi

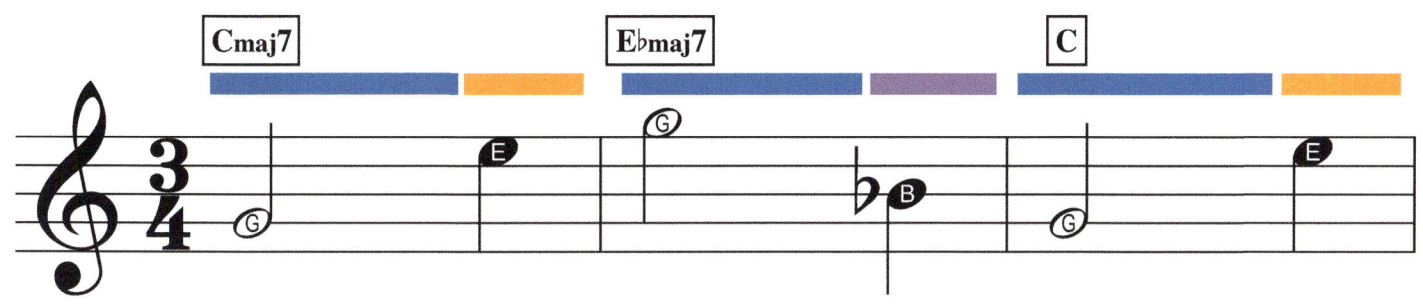
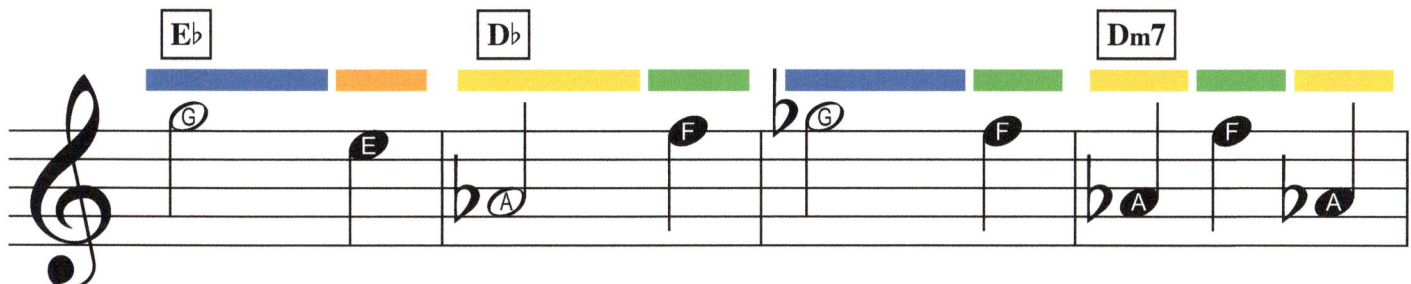
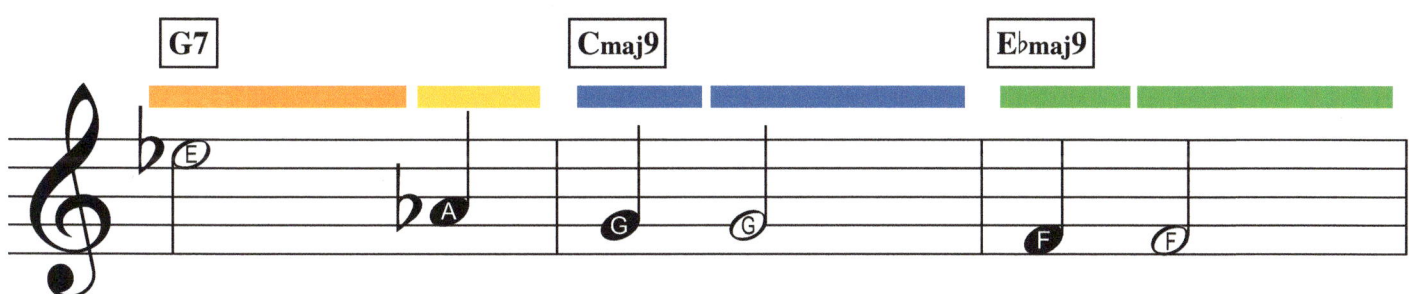
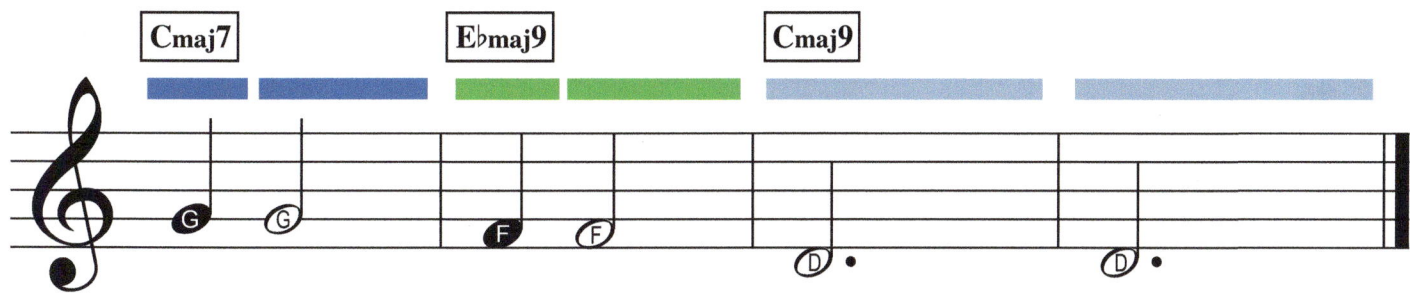

Copyright © 1967 LEE MENDELSON FILM PRODUCTIONS, INC.
Copyright Renewed
International Copyright Secured   All Rights Reserved

Sharp or Flat?

Placing a sharp in front of a note raises the pitch a half step. Add sharps to these notes. Be sure to place the sharp sign in front of the note. The "center square" of the sharp sign includes the line or space of the note.

Placing a flat in front of a note lowers the pitch a half step. Add flat signs to these notes. Place the round part of the flat sign carefully to include the line or space of the note.

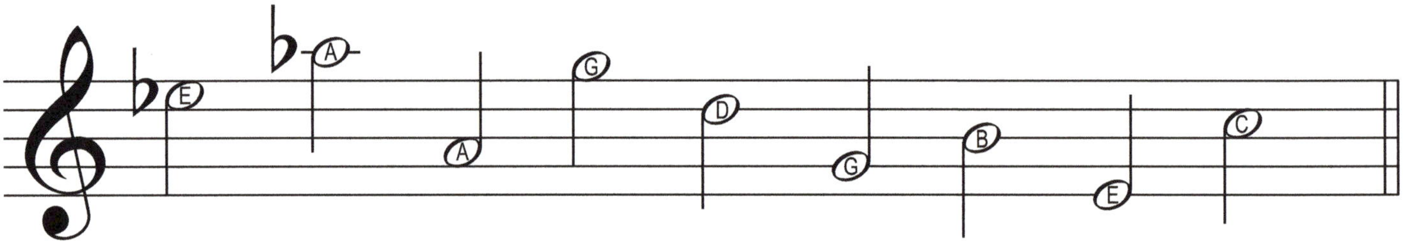

Name the following sharp and flat notes.

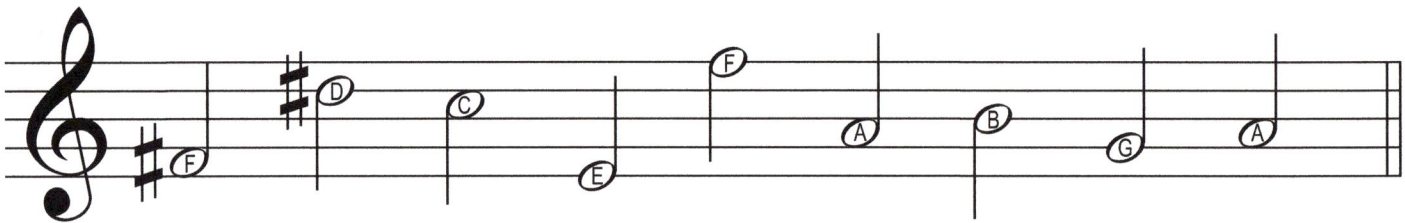

1. ____ 2. ____ 3. ____ 4. ____ 5. ____

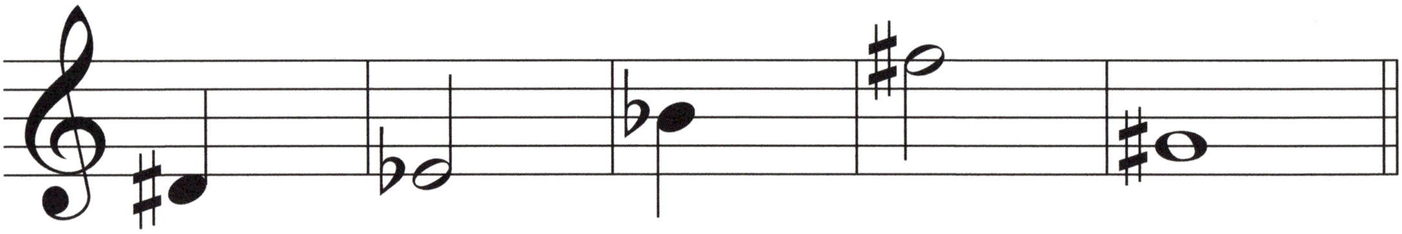

6. ____ 7. ____ 8. ____ 9. ____ 10. ____

Answers on page 96.

Ties

Earlier in the book you learned that a whole note is our longest note, and that it lasts four beats. Then how do composers write longer notes? They use *ties*. Ties are curved lines that connect two or more of the same note name to make longer notes. The tied notes must be on the same line or in the same space. The first note is played or sung and held for the full value of all the tied notes. Play and count the example below.

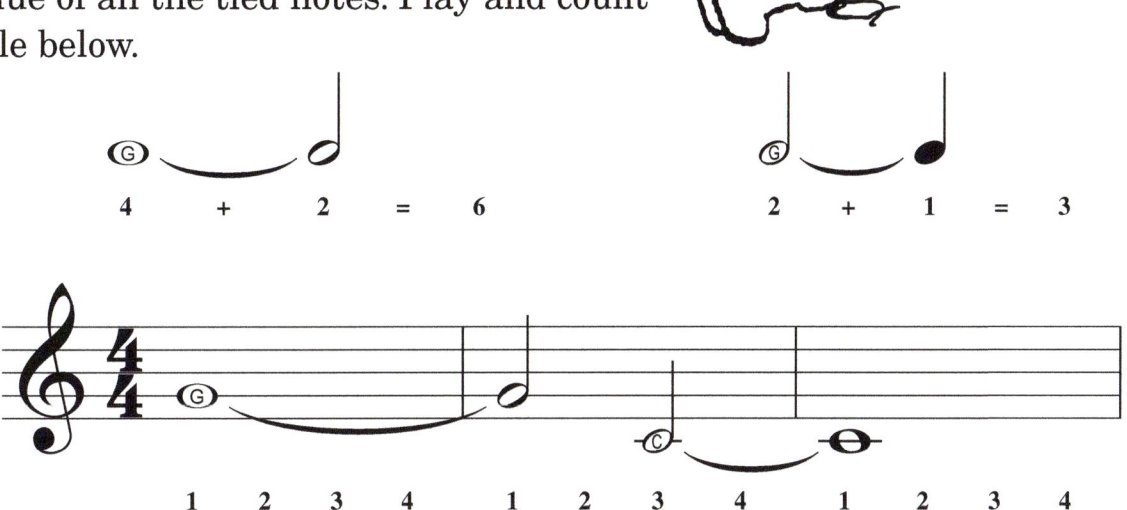

1st and 2nd Endings

"Baseball Theme" on page 40 uses the repeat sign in a different way. Sometimes a whole section of music can be repeated, ending in a slightly different way the second time. This is indicated by *1st and 2nd ending* signs. Play from the beginning to the repeat sign. The measures leading up to the repeat sign are marked with a first ending sign. Now go back to the first repeat sign. Play these measures again, but skip the first ending and play the second ending measures. 1st and 2nd ending signs look like this:

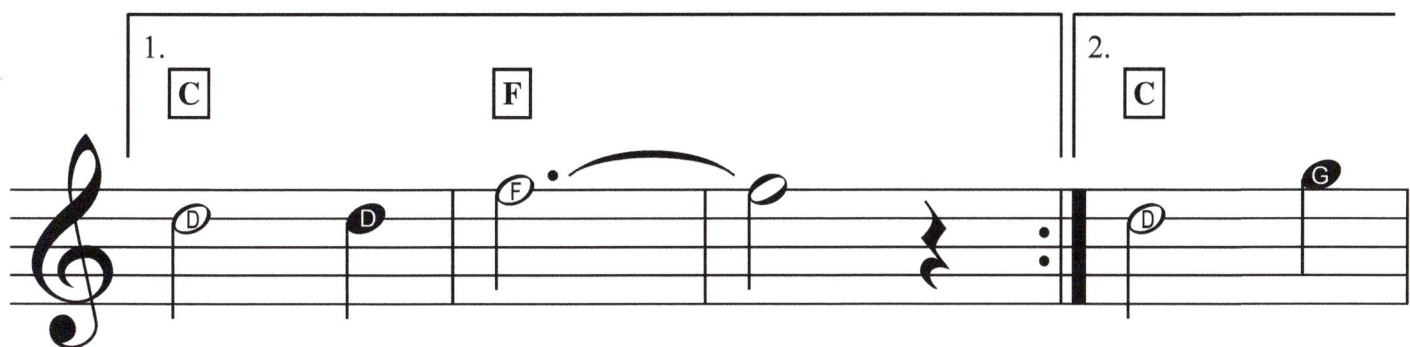

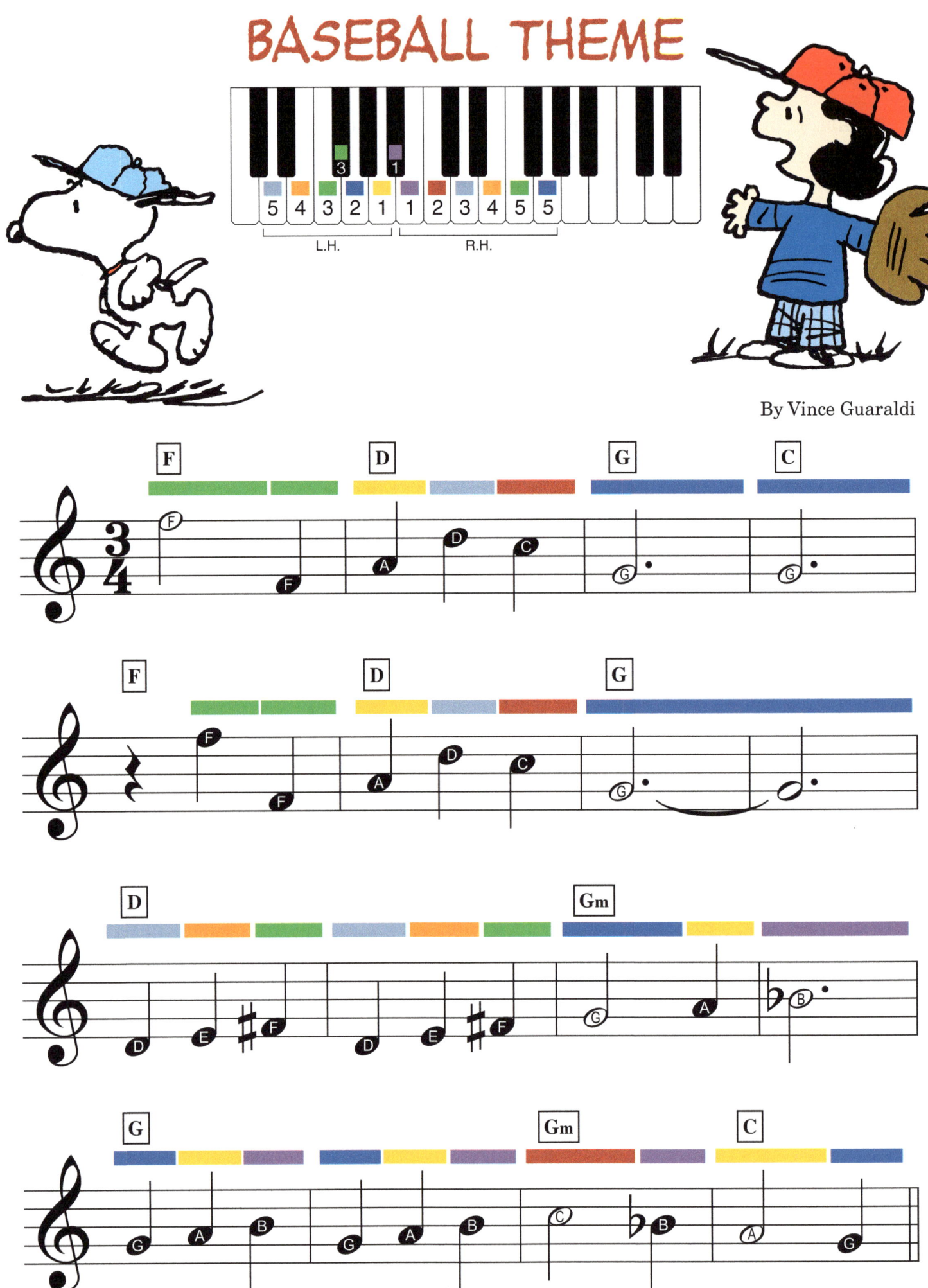

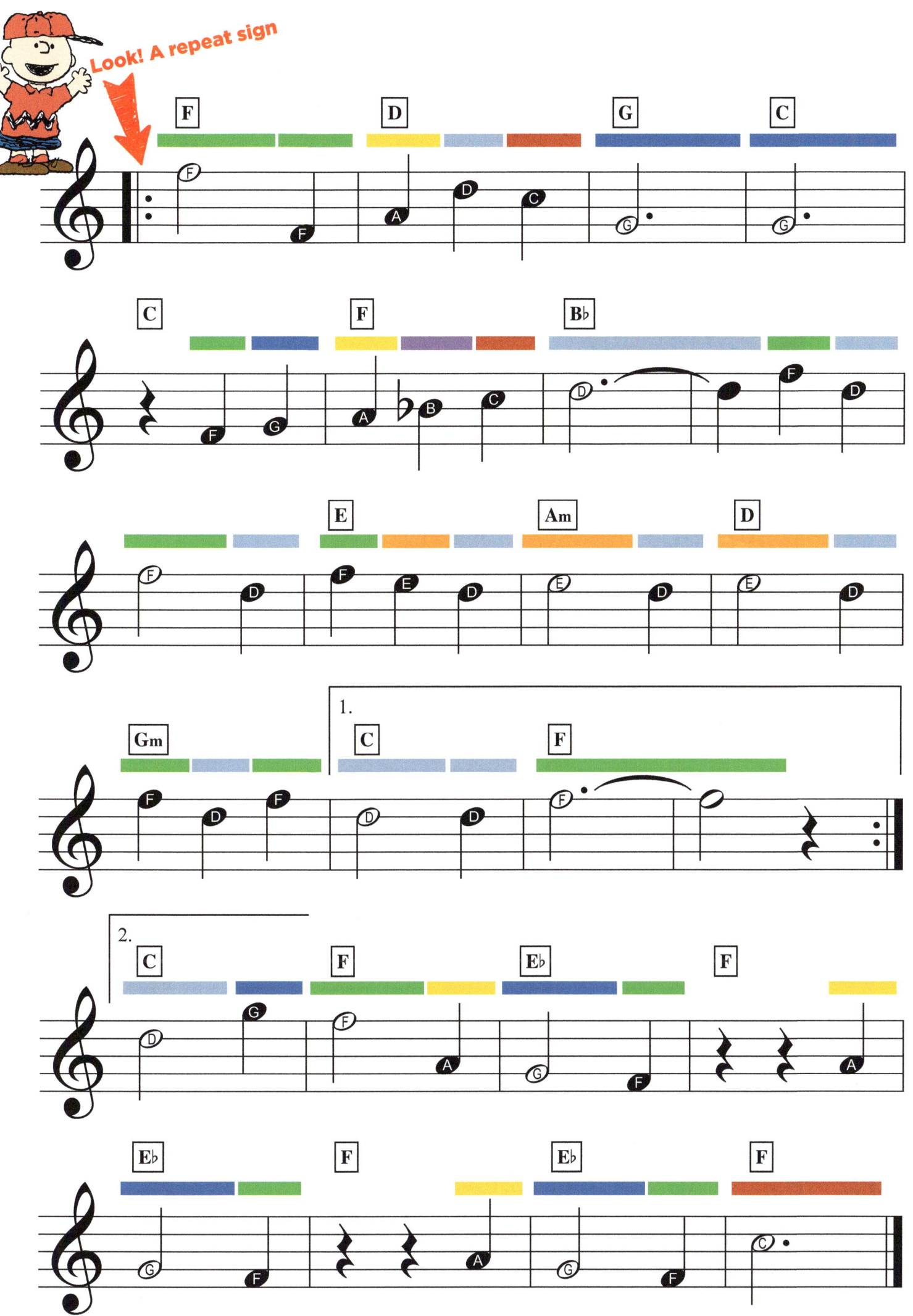

More About Sharps and Flats

Sharps and flats create more notes to play in our songs. Let's review these important musical symbols.

A sharp ♯ *raises* a note. On the keyboard, this is the very next note higher, usually a black key.

A flat ♭ *lowers* a note. On the keyboard, this is the very next note lower, usually a black key.

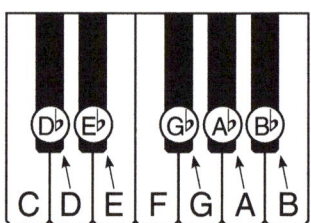

Here's a new rule. Notes that are sharp or flat **stay sharp or flat for the whole measure**.

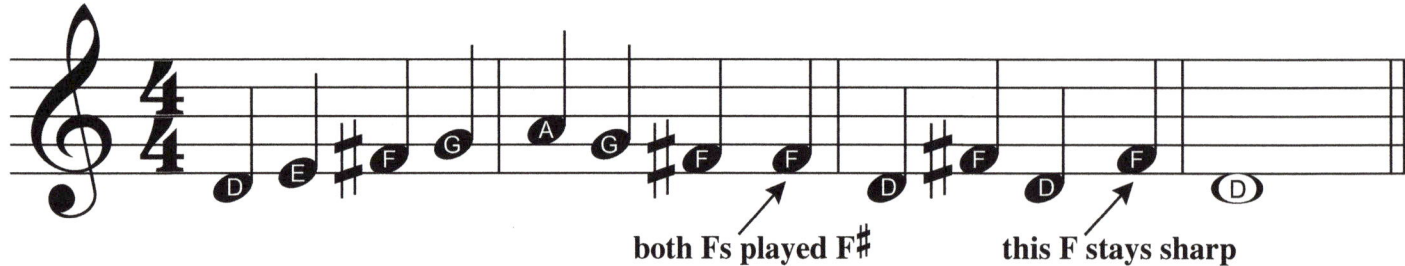

both Fs played F♯   **this F stays sharp**

To cancel a sharp or flat, use this new symbol called a *natural*: ♮

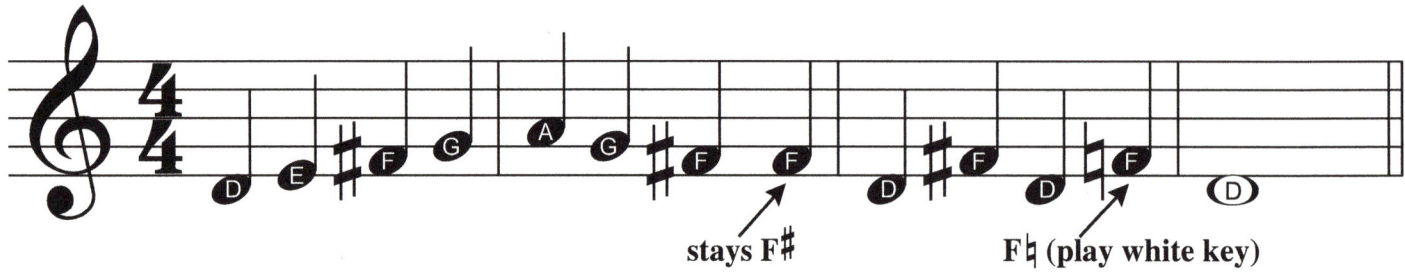

stays F♯   **F♮ (play white key)**

Music Math

Let's do some music math! Add the values of the tied notes to find the answer to each of these musical equations. The first one is done for you. Check your answers on page 96.

1.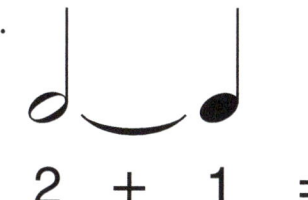
   <u> 2 </u> + <u> 1 </u> = <u> 3 </u>

2.
   ___ + ___ + ___ = ___

3.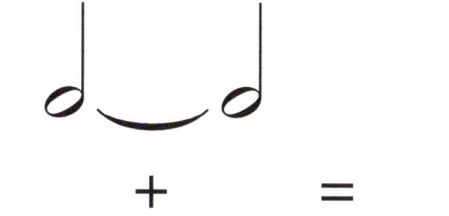
   ___ + ___ = ___

4.
   ___ + ___ + ___ = ___

5.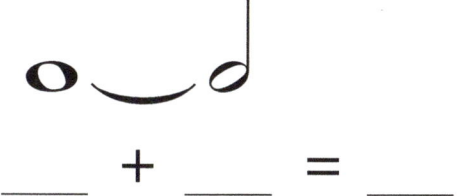
   ___ + ___ = ___

6.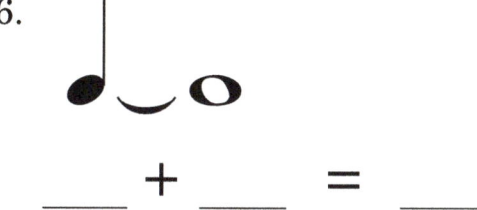
   ___ + ___ = ___

7.
   ___ + ___ + ___ = ___

8.
   ___ + ___ = ___

9.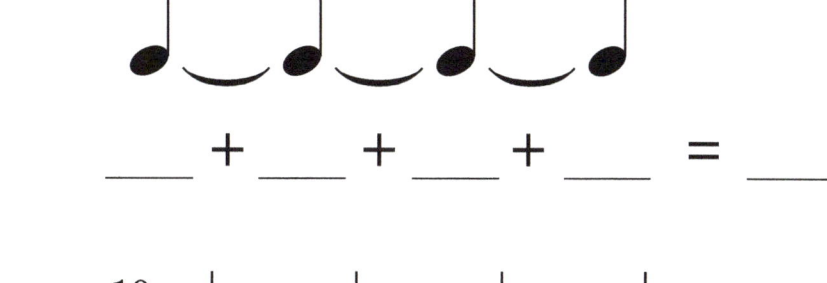
   ___ + ___ + ___ + ___ = ___

10.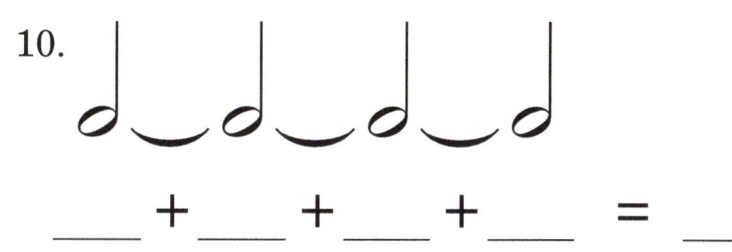
    ___ + ___ + ___ + ___ = ___

Eighth Notes

Music uses many different kinds of notes. So far, you've learned about quarter notes, half notes, dotted half notes, and whole notes. Here's something new: eighth notes!

One eighth note looks like a quarter note with a flag. When two or more eighth notes appear together, the flags turn into beams. When the time signature is $\frac{4}{4}$ eighth notes are often connected in groups of two or four. The beams make reading the eighth notes easier.

Practice drawing some flags and beams.
The first example in each line is done for you.

Counting Eighth Notes

Remember when we used a pizza to show the value of notes? One whole pizza was like a whole note. When we cut the pizza in half, we could see two half notes. Then we divided each half into quarters. If we divide the pizza one more time, we'll divide the four quarter notes into eight eighth notes. We'll also have eight pieces of pizza.

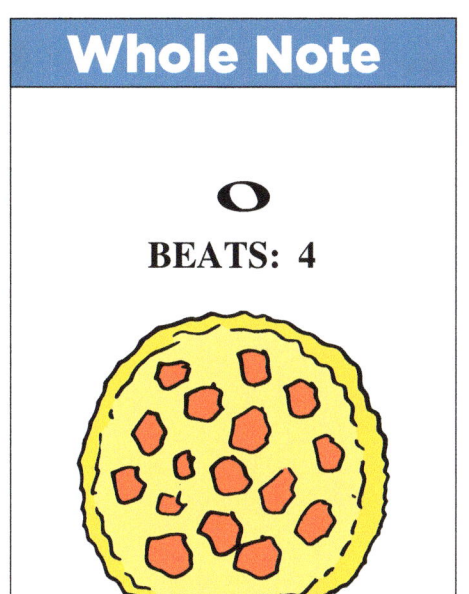

Whole Note

BEATS: 4

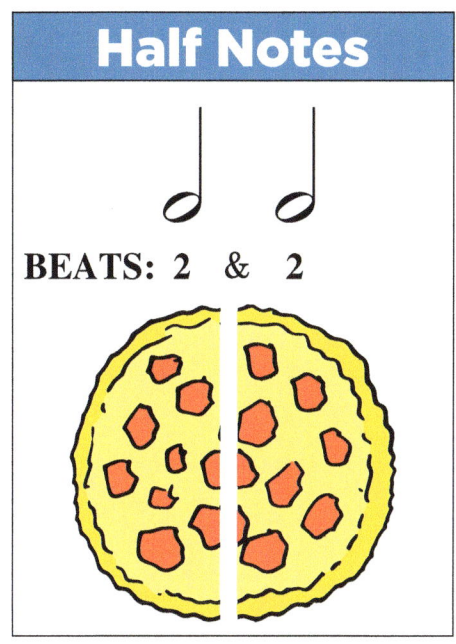

Half Notes

BEATS: 2 & 2

Quarter Notes

BEATS: 1 & 1 & 1 & 1

Eighth Notes

BEATS: 1 & 1 & 1 & 1 &

When you count eighth notes and half beats, it's easier if you think about tapping your foot to the music. Look at Charlie Brown's shoe, tapping along with the quarter notes. We count the quarter notes 1-2-3-4.

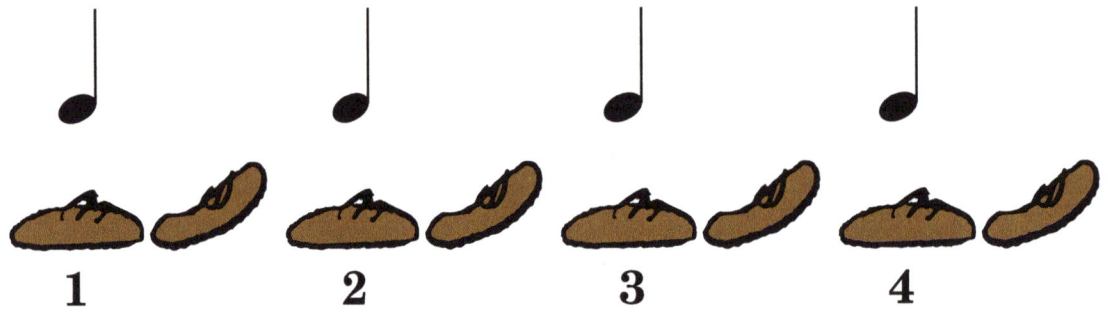

As he taps, his foot moves up and down, tapping on the floor for each quarter note beat. To count eighth notes, he taps the same way but the notes sound twice as fast. Two eighth notes equal one quarter note.

Count: 1 & 2 & 3 & 4 &

The "ands" are when he raises his foot.

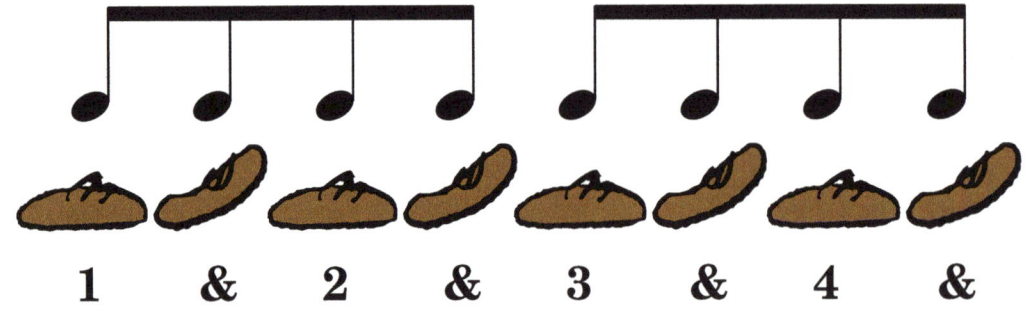

Try it yourself, tapping your foot and counting 1 & 2 & 3 & 4 &

Fermata

A fermata sign over a note means to hold a note longer than its rhythmic value.

HAPPY BIRTHDAY TO YOU

Words and Music by Mildred J. Hill and Patty S. Hill

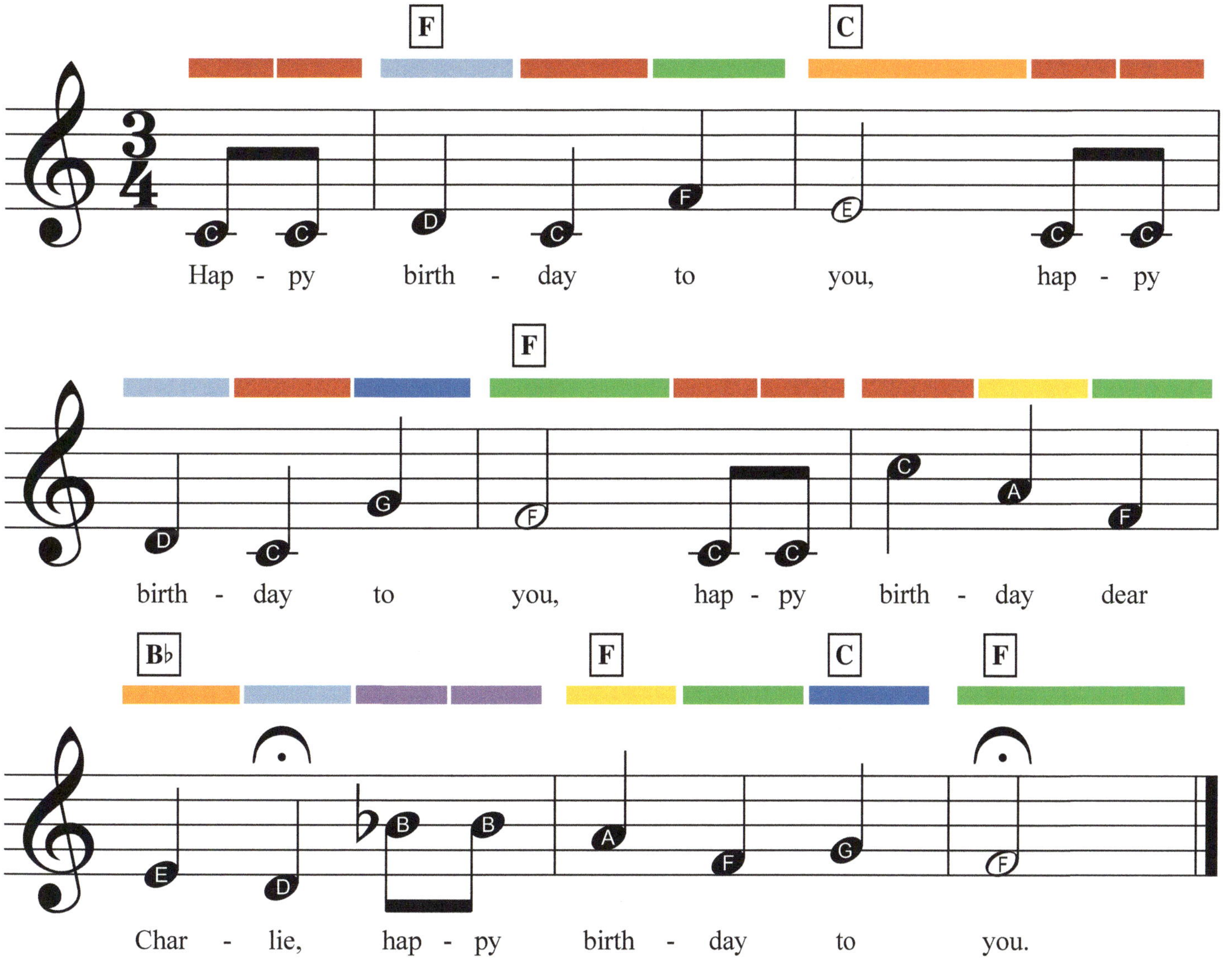

| F | C |
Hap-py birth-day to you, hap-py
C C D C F E C C

| F |
birth-day to you, hap-py birth-day dear
D C G F C C A F

| B♭ | F | C | F |
Char-lie, hap-py birth-day to you.
E D B♭ B A F G F

© 1935 (Renewed) SUMMY-BIRCHARD MUSIC, a Division of SUMMY-BIRCHARD INC.
All Rights Administered by WB MUSIC CORP.
All Rights for Europe Controlled and Administered by KEITH PROWSE MUSIC CO.
All Rights Reserved   Used by Permission

Here are some rhythms to practice.
Don't forget to count and tap your foot.

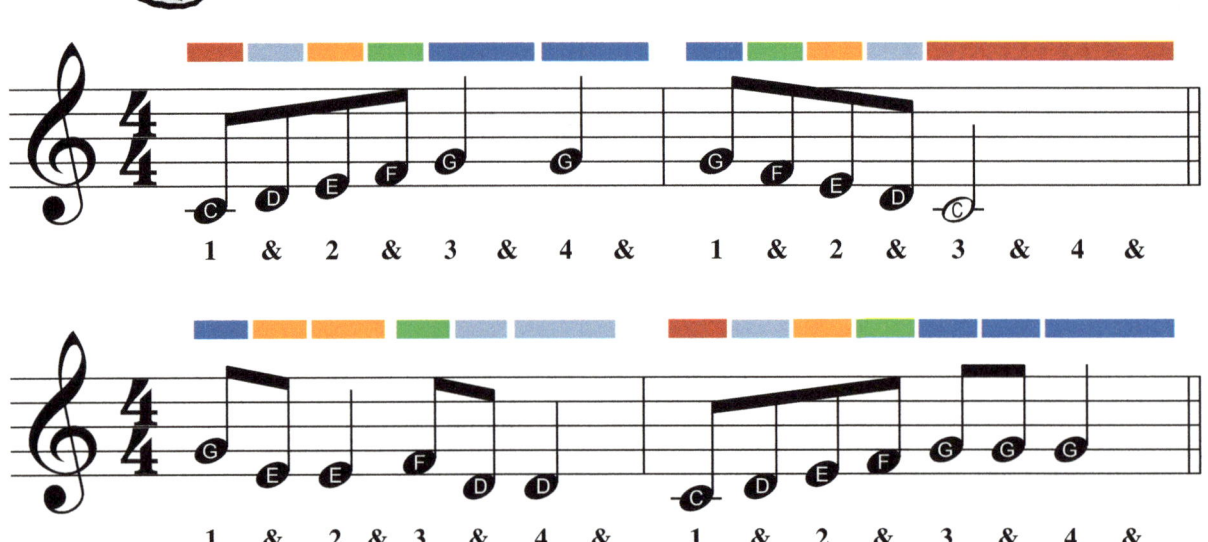

Eighth Rests

You know what rests are: symbols for silence, or places you don't play any notes. An eighth rest lasts as long as an eighth note: half a beat. It looks like this:

Practice clapping and counting some rhythms with eighth rests.

Rhythm Word Search

Find the hidden rhythm words.

Y	O	J	H	K	U	O	W	D	V	Y	W	K	E	L
R	E	B	A	R	L	I	N	E	M	U	H	T	Z	J
M	R	W	S	X	T	N	S	Q	T	S	O	E	K	A
P	E	R	U	S	V	R	I	B	U	E	L	R	B	W
W	P	T	E	G	U	B	N	E	T	A	E	H	V	M
X	P	R	E	H	F	N	N	A	M	N	R	Y	I	X
O	A	M	S	R	L	X	T	T	W	O	J	T	M	B
L	Z	R	U	M	X	O	F	Z	Z	T	V	H	E	U
G	V	Y	S	W	N	N	N	F	O	E	B	M	G	R
I	Z	Q	M	E	A	S	U	R	E	V	N	Y	V	C
L	T	I	M	E	S	I	G	N	A	T	U	R	E	G
G	A	H	G	E	V	Q	R	S	X	E	H	Z	V	S

bar line
beat
measure
notate
note
quarter
rest
rhythm
time signature
whole
meter

Time for a Rest

Match the following rests to the correct name.

half rest

eighth rest

whole rest

quarter rest

Answers on page 96.

"Happiness Theme" will give you a good chance to practice playing eighth notes. Tap your foot and clap the rhythms before you play the notes on the keyboard. Notice you start with pick-up notes, and hold all tied notes for their full value.

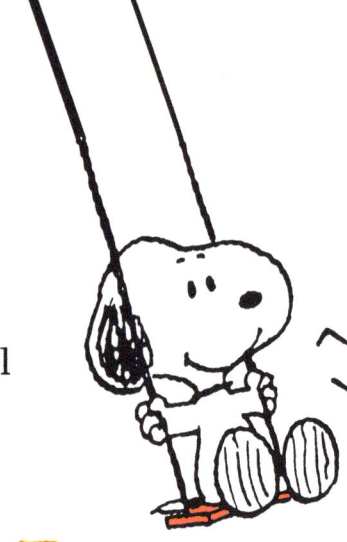

HAPPINESS THEME

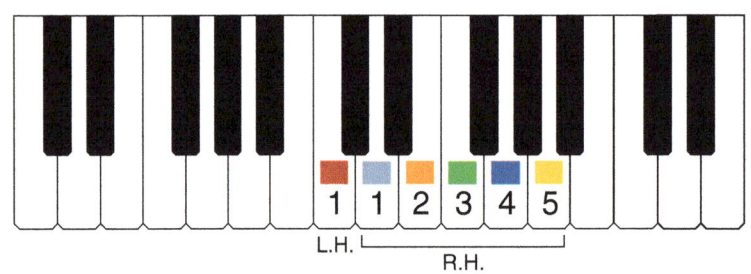

By Vince Guaraldi

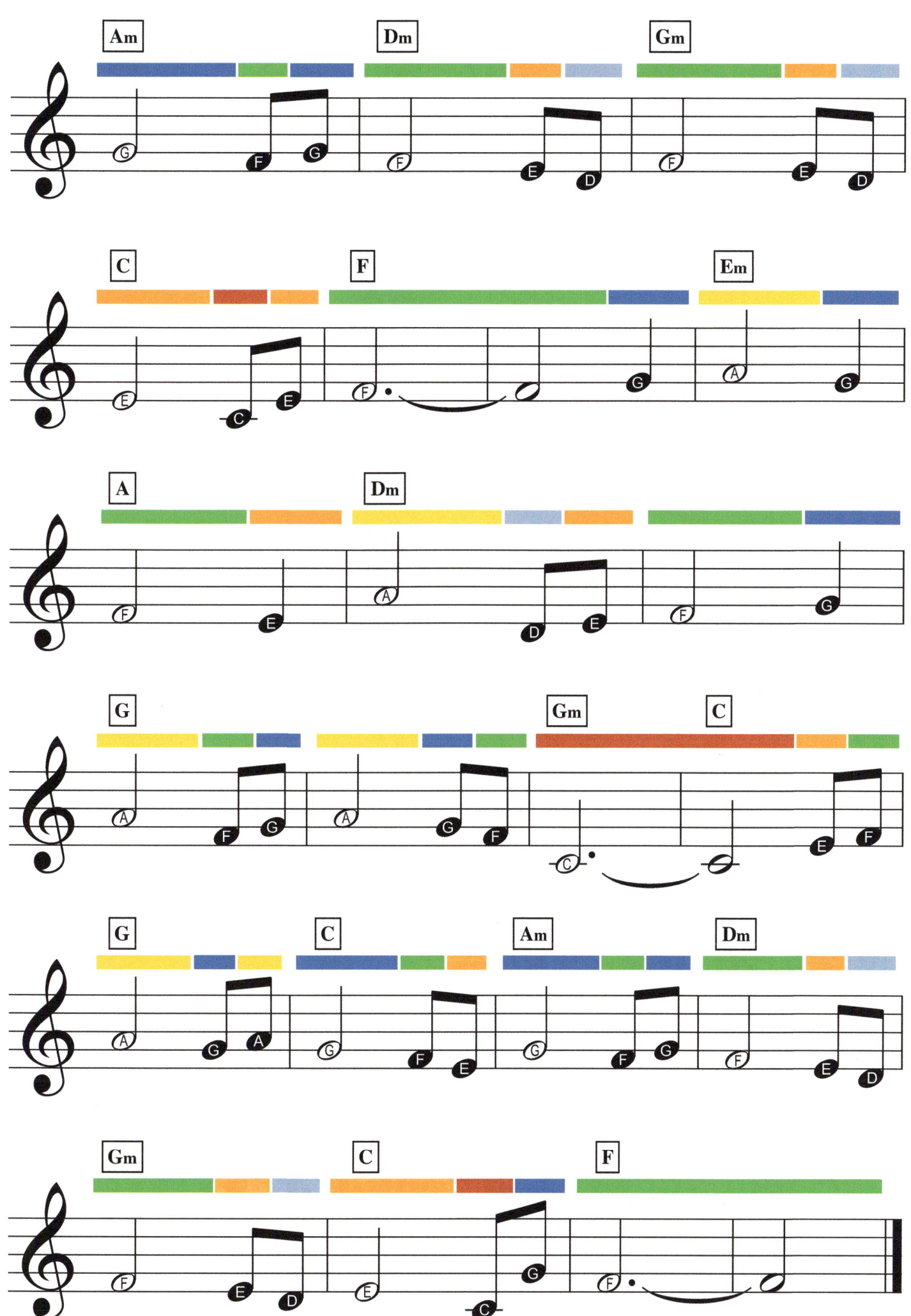

Can you find the skips in this song? Remember, skips are notes that are written on the staff from a line to a line, or a space to a space. Knowing where the skips are will help you play this song. Keep the quarter notes steady, and the eighth notes smooth. Remember, eighth notes are twice as fast as quarter notes.

RED BARON

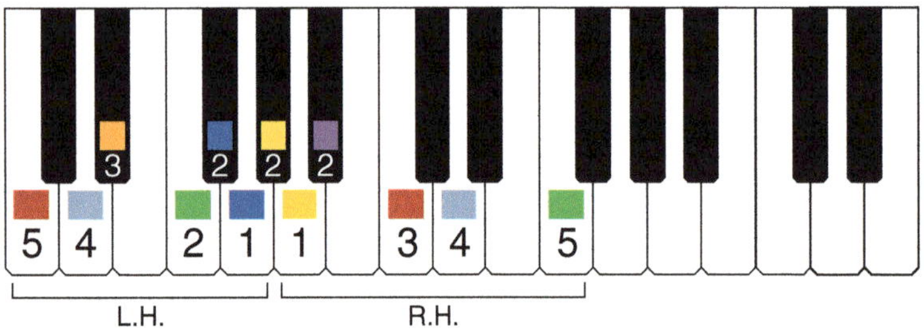

By Vince Guaraldi

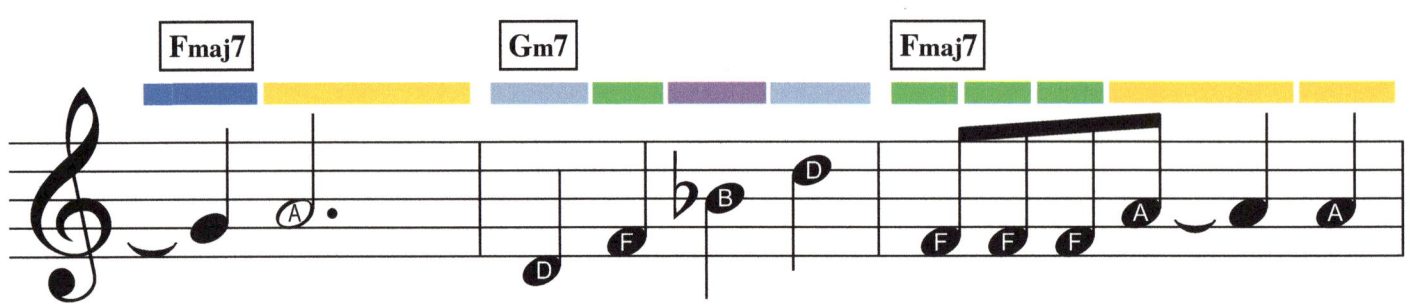

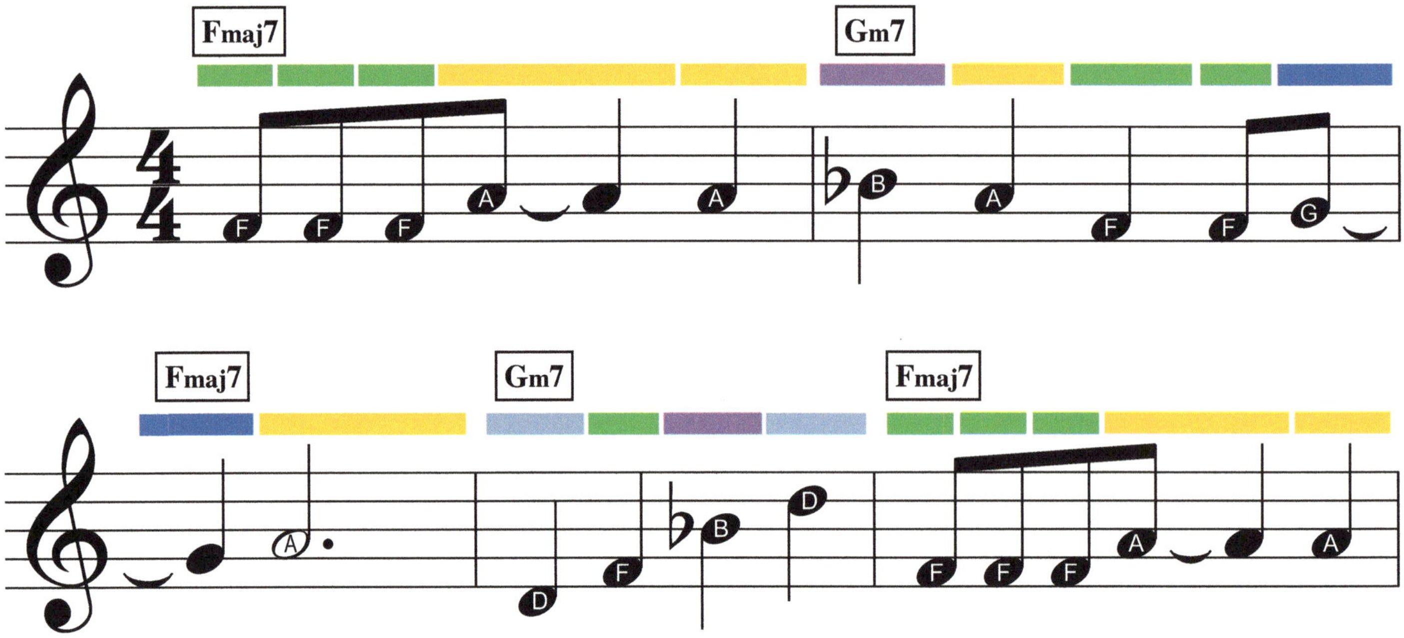

Copyright © 1966 LEE MENDELSON FILM PRODUCTIONS, INC.
Copyright Renewed
International Copyright Secured   All Rights Reserved

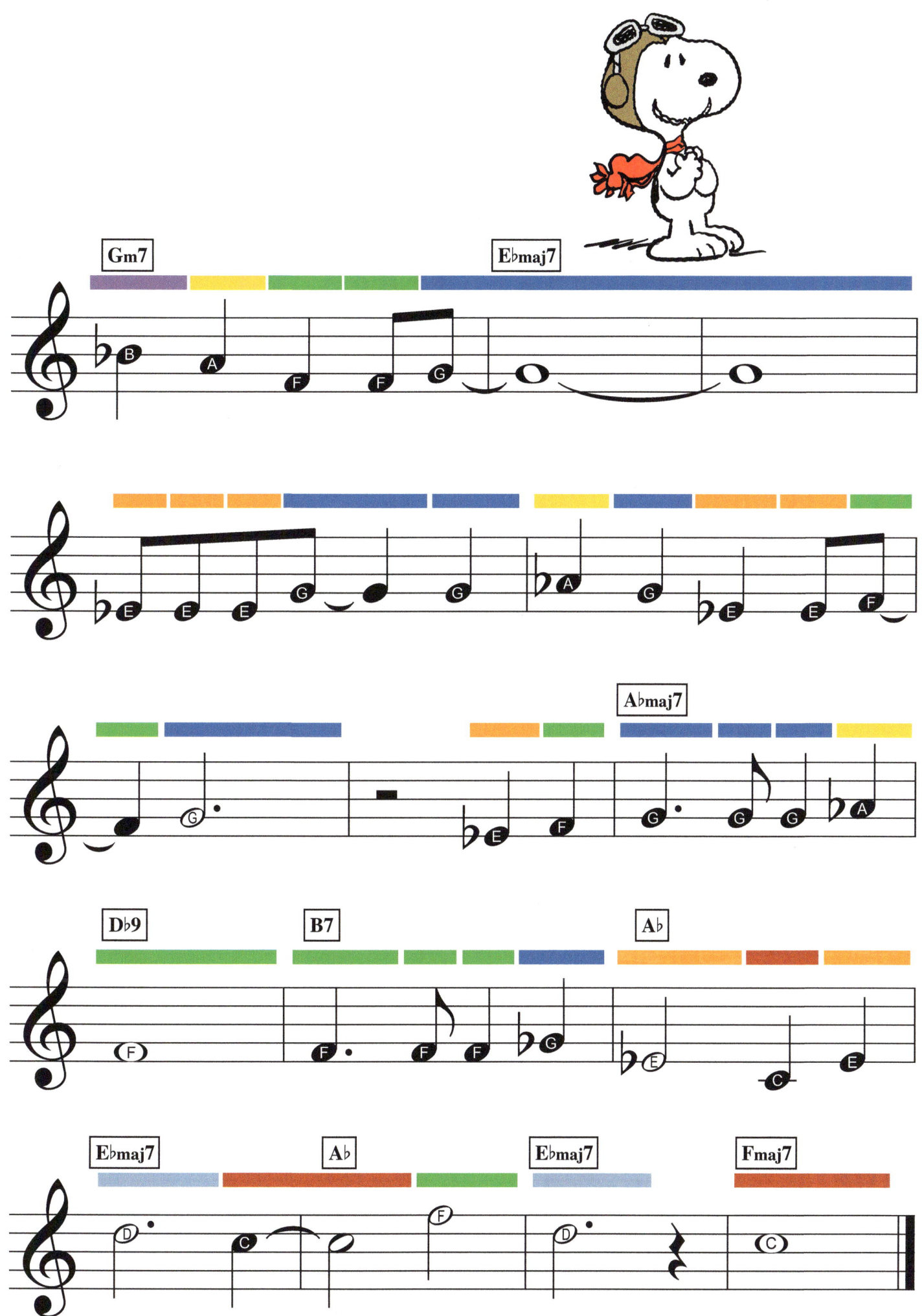

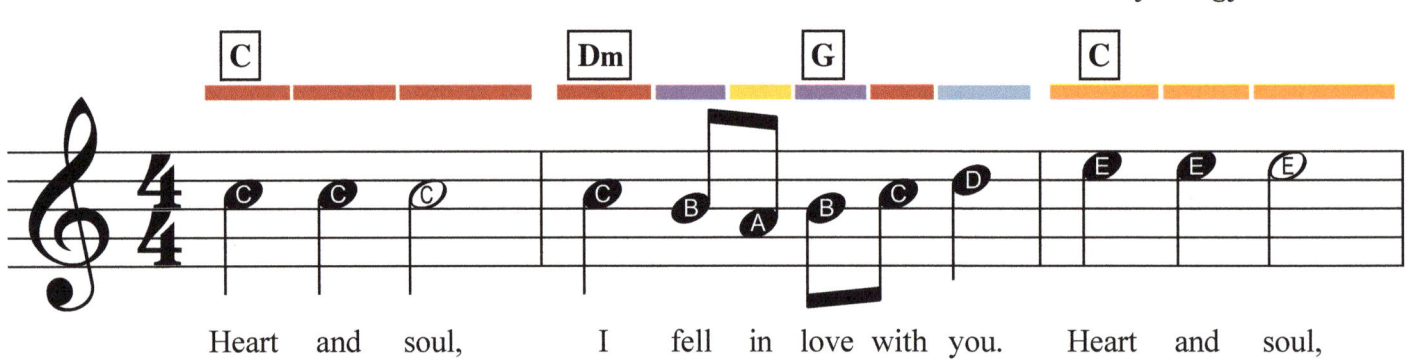

from the Paramount Short Subject A SONG IS BORN
Words by Frank Loesser
Music by Hoagy Carmichael

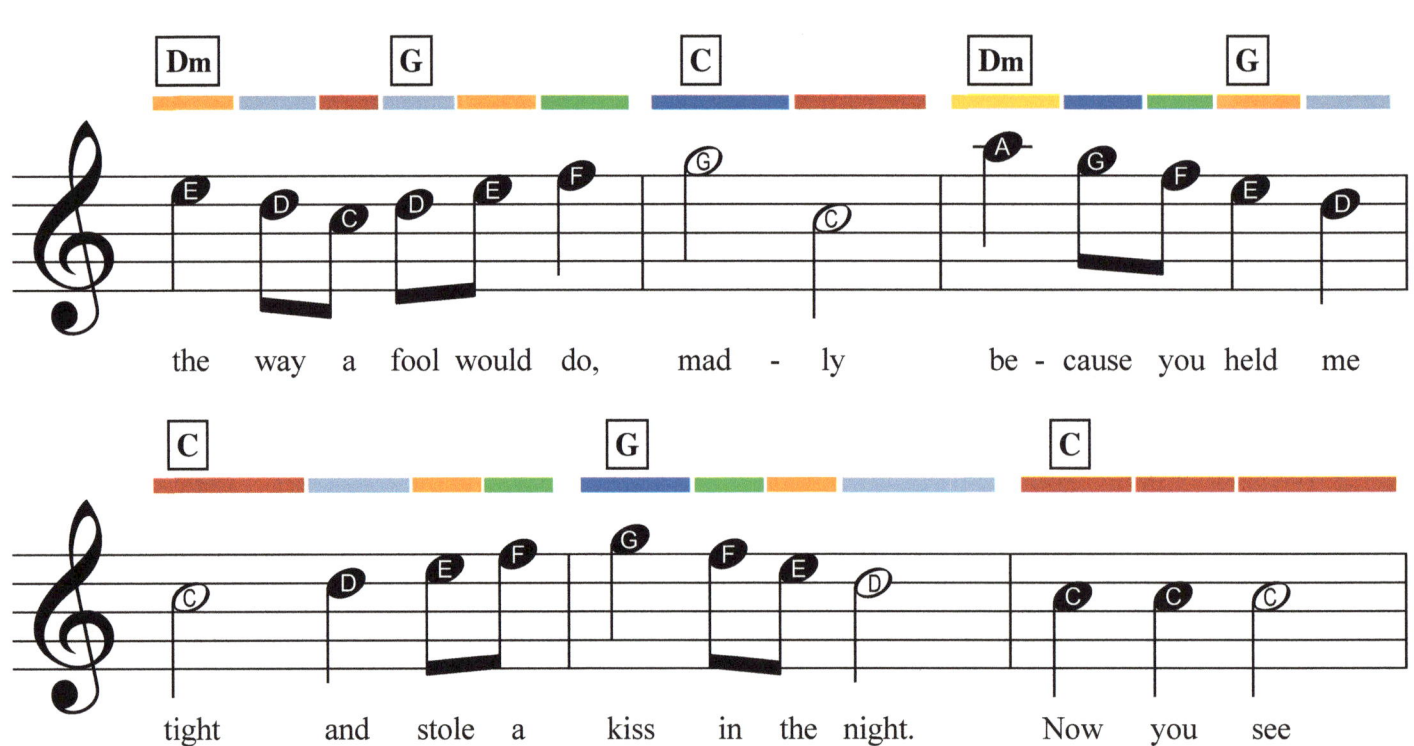

Copyright © 1938 Sony/ATV Music Publishing LLC
Copyright Renewed
All Rights Administered by Sony/ATV Music Publishing LLC, 424 Church Street, Suite 1200, Nashville, TN 37219
International Copyright Secured   All Rights Reserved

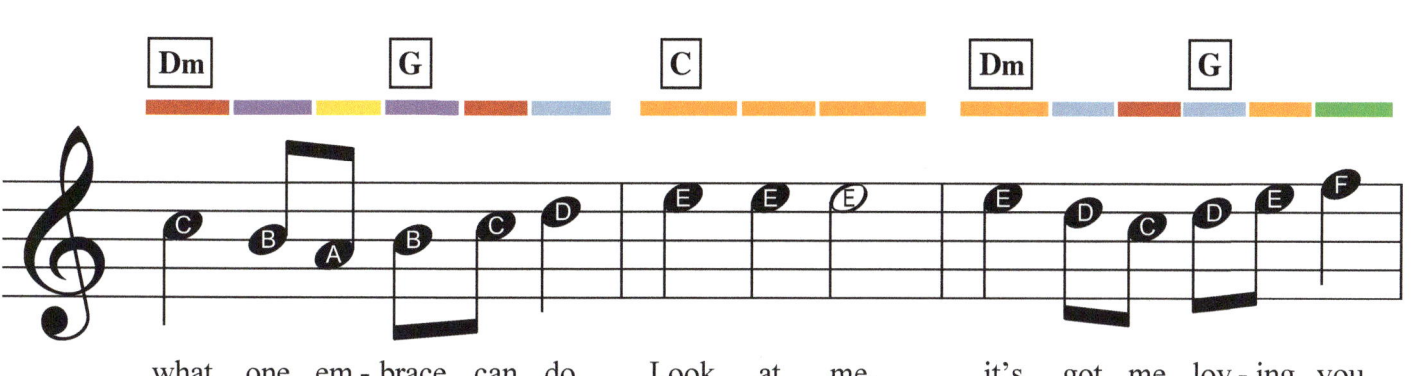

what one em-brace can do. Look at me, it's got me lov-ing you,

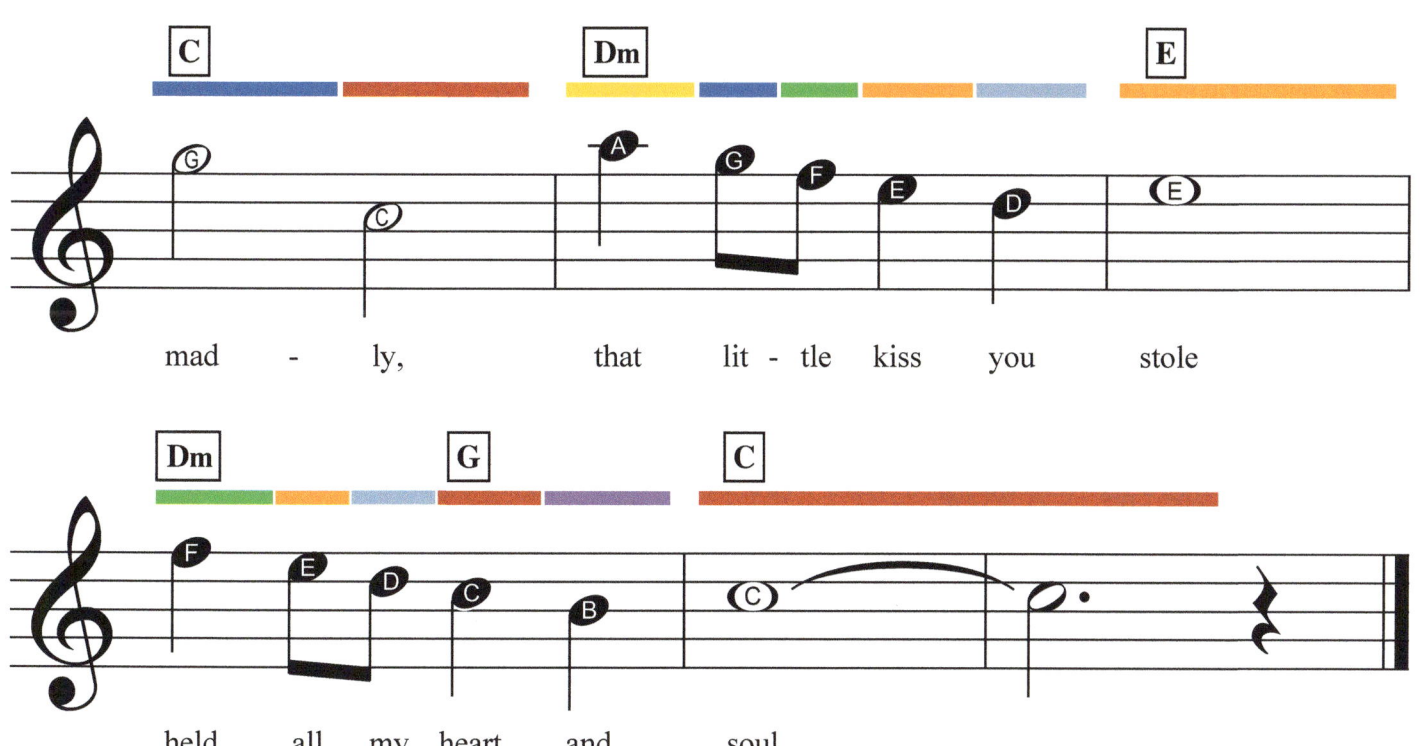

mad - ly, that lit - tle kiss you stole

held all my heart and soul. _____

THIS LAND IS YOUR LAND

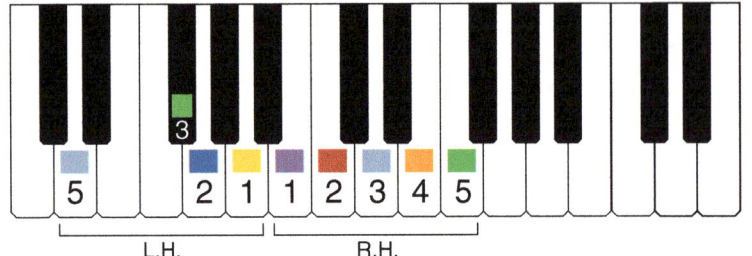

Words and Music by Woody Guthrie

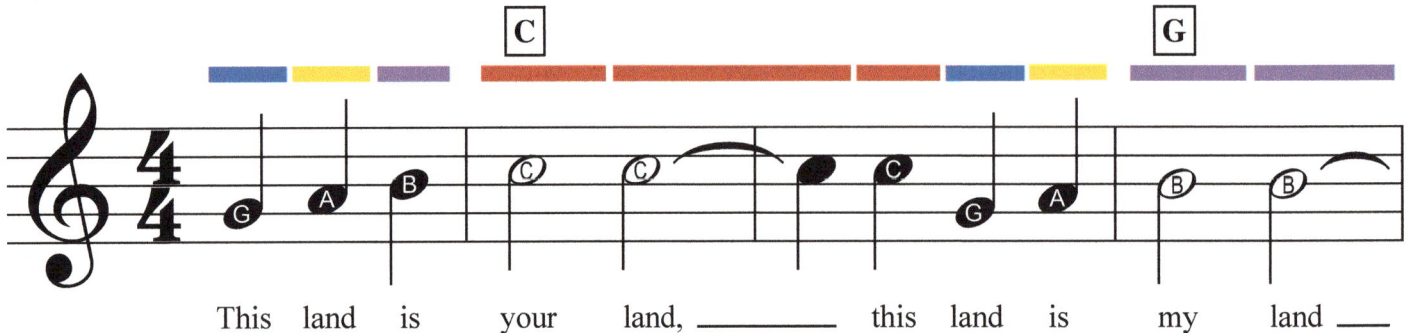

This land is your land, _____ this land is my land _____

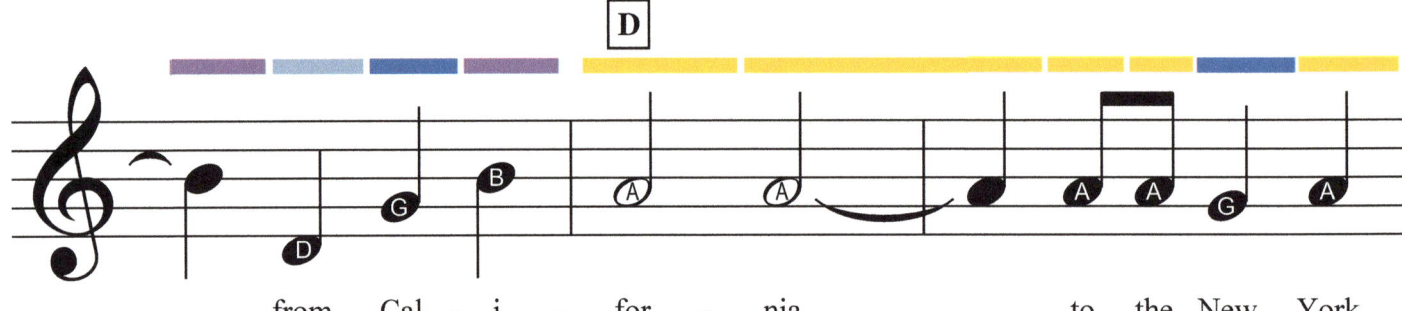

_____ from Cal - i - for - nia _____ to the New York

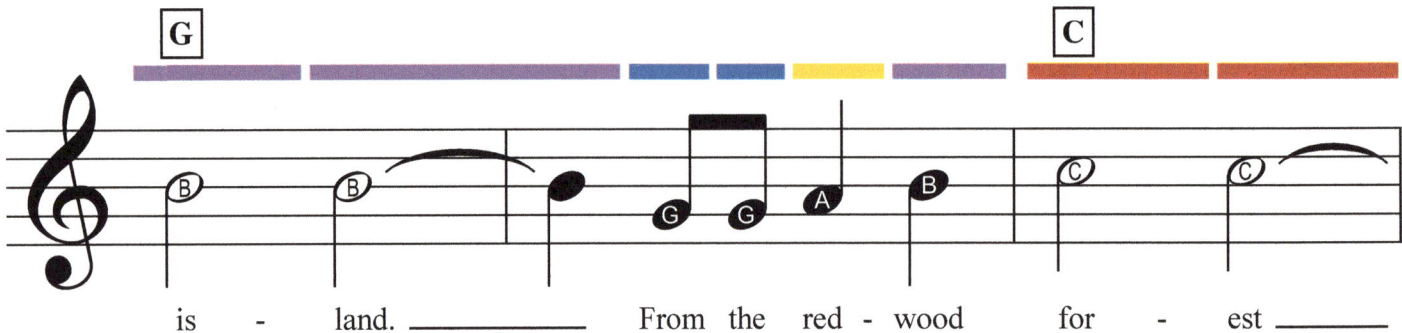

is - land. _____ From the red - wood for - est _____

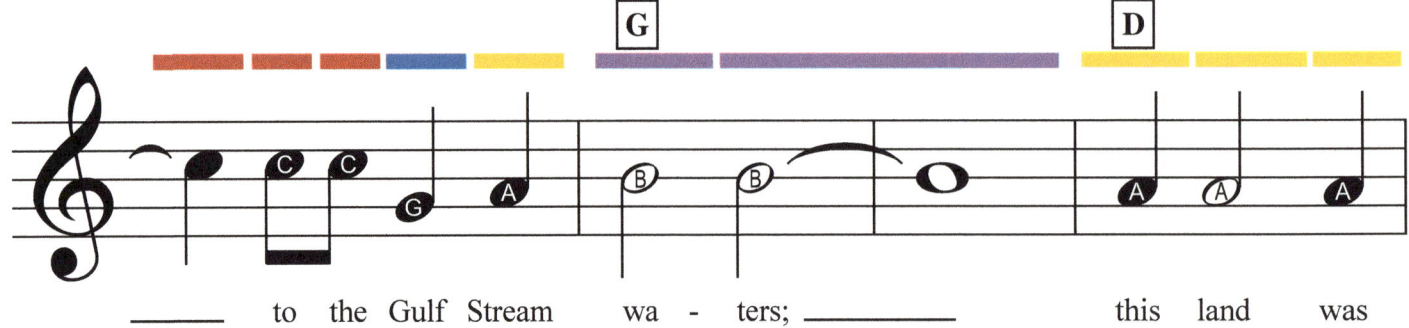

_____ to the Gulf Stream wa - ters; _____ this land was

WGP/TRO - © Copyright 1956, 1958, 1970, 1972 (Copyrights Renewed) Woody Guthrie Publications, Inc. & Ludlow Music, Inc., New York, NY
administered by Ludlow Music, Inc.
International Copyright Secured
All Rights Reserved Including Public Performance For Profit
Used by Permission

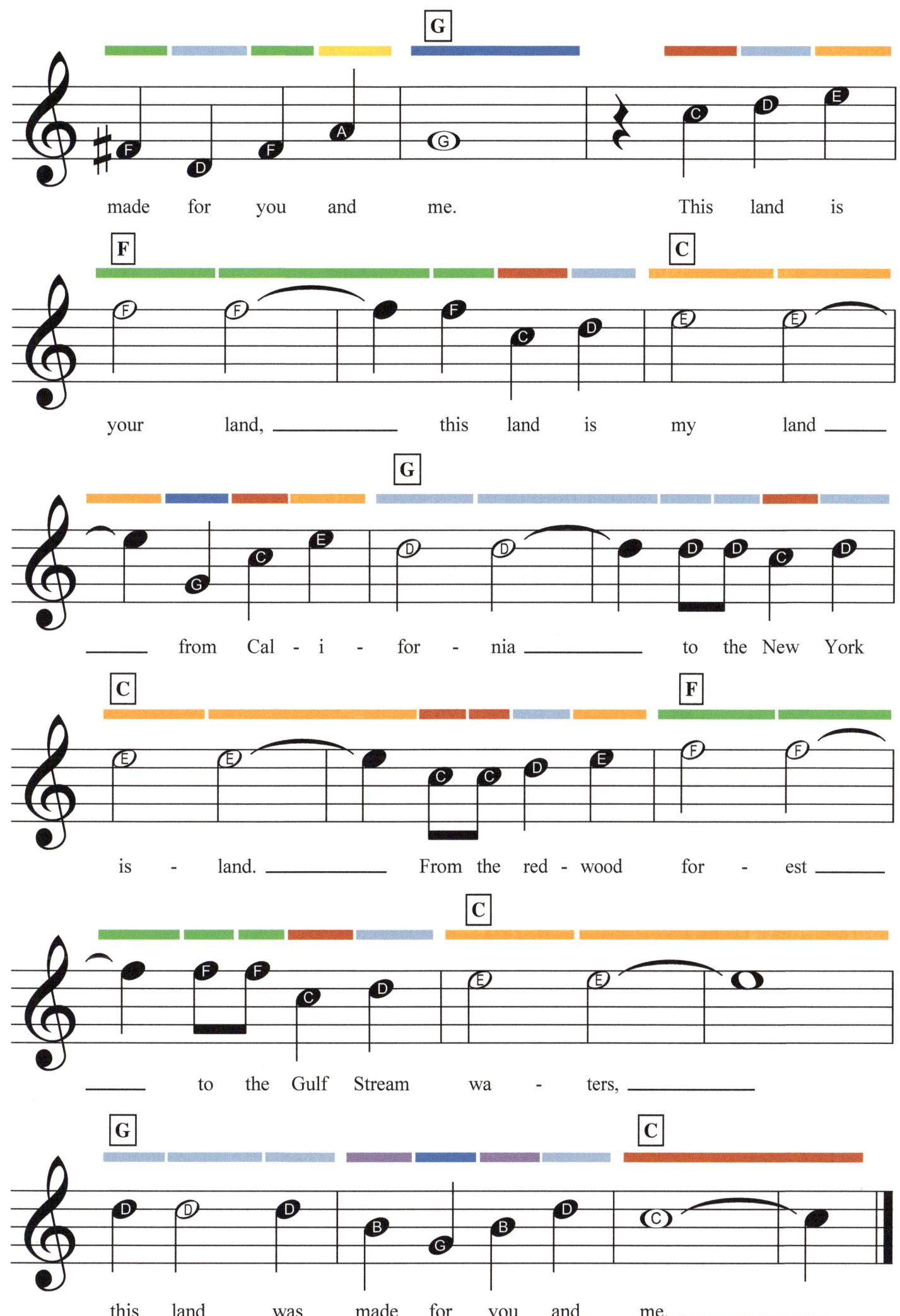

Dotted Notes

You know that a dotted half note equals three beats. The dot adds half the value of the note it follows. It's kind of like playing a tied note without the tie.

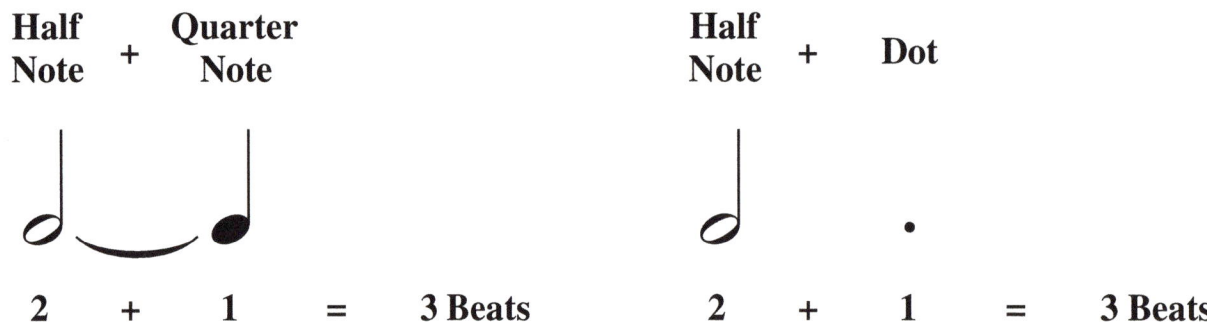

You can add a dot to any note to increase its value. When you add a dot to a quarter note, you add half a beat.

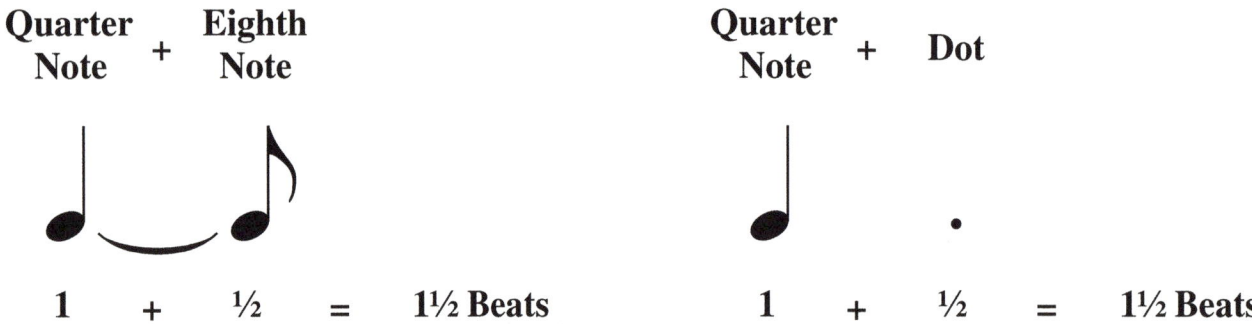

A dotted quarter note is often followed by an eighth note. Here are some dotted note rhythms to practice. Clap and count. You may wish to tap your foot to keep the beat.

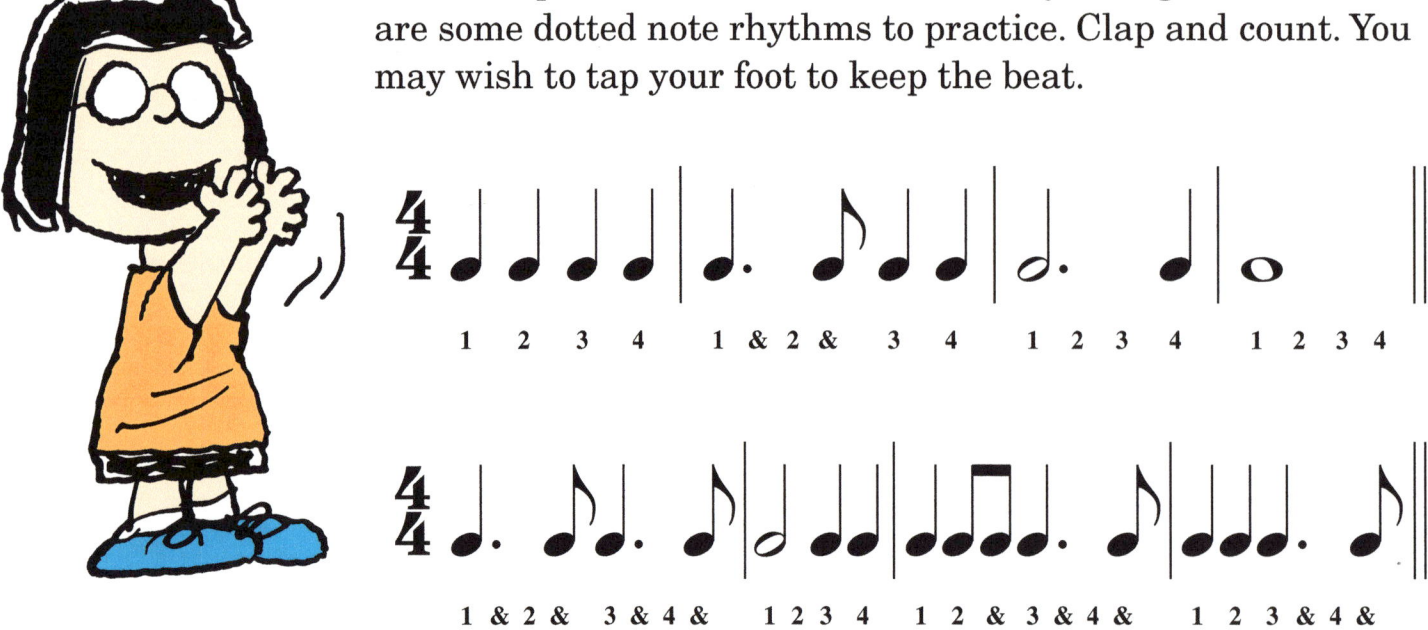

Note Matching

Draw a line from the note on the left to the pizza on the right that represents the same number of beats. The answers are on page 96.

DOTTED HALF NOTE		4 BEATS
DOTTED QUARTER NOTE		3 BEATS
HALF NOTE		2 BEATS
WHOLE NOTE		1-1/2 BEATS
EIGHTH NOTE		1 BEAT
QUARTER NOTE		1/2 BEAT

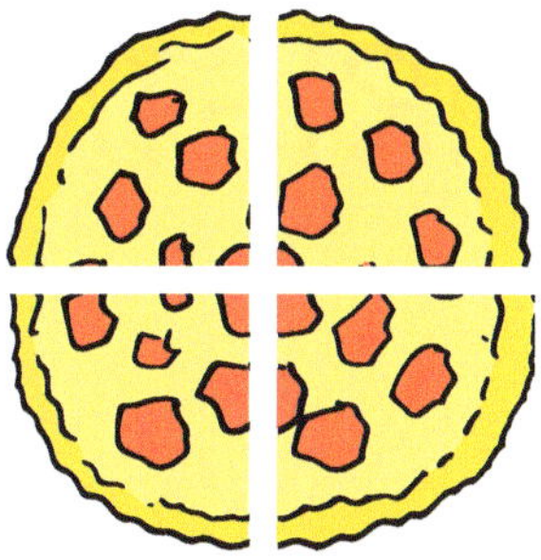

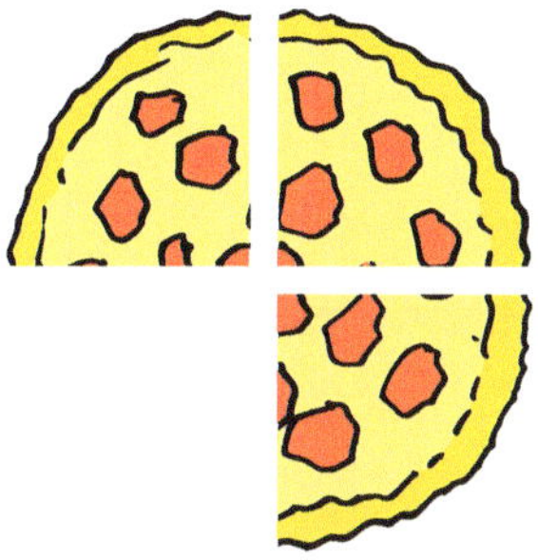

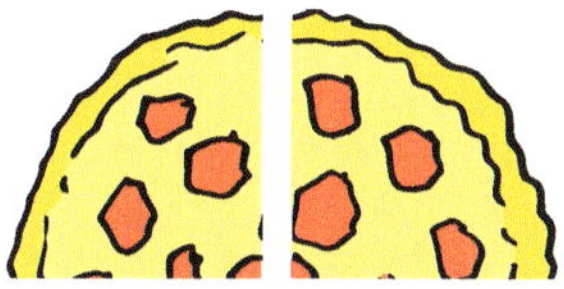

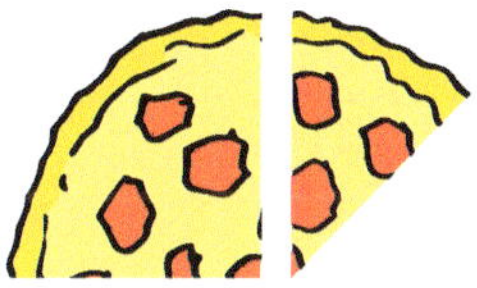

CHRISTMAS TIME IS HERE

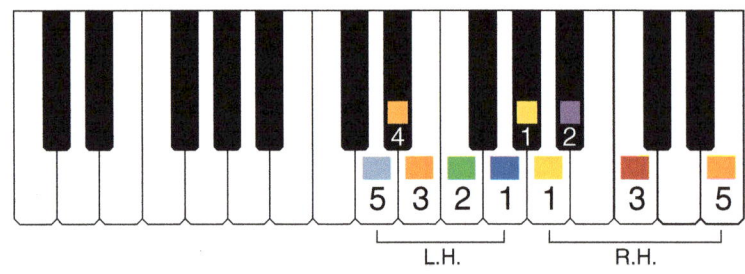

from A CHARLIE BROWN CHRISTMAS
Words by Lee Mendelson
Music by Vince Guaraldi

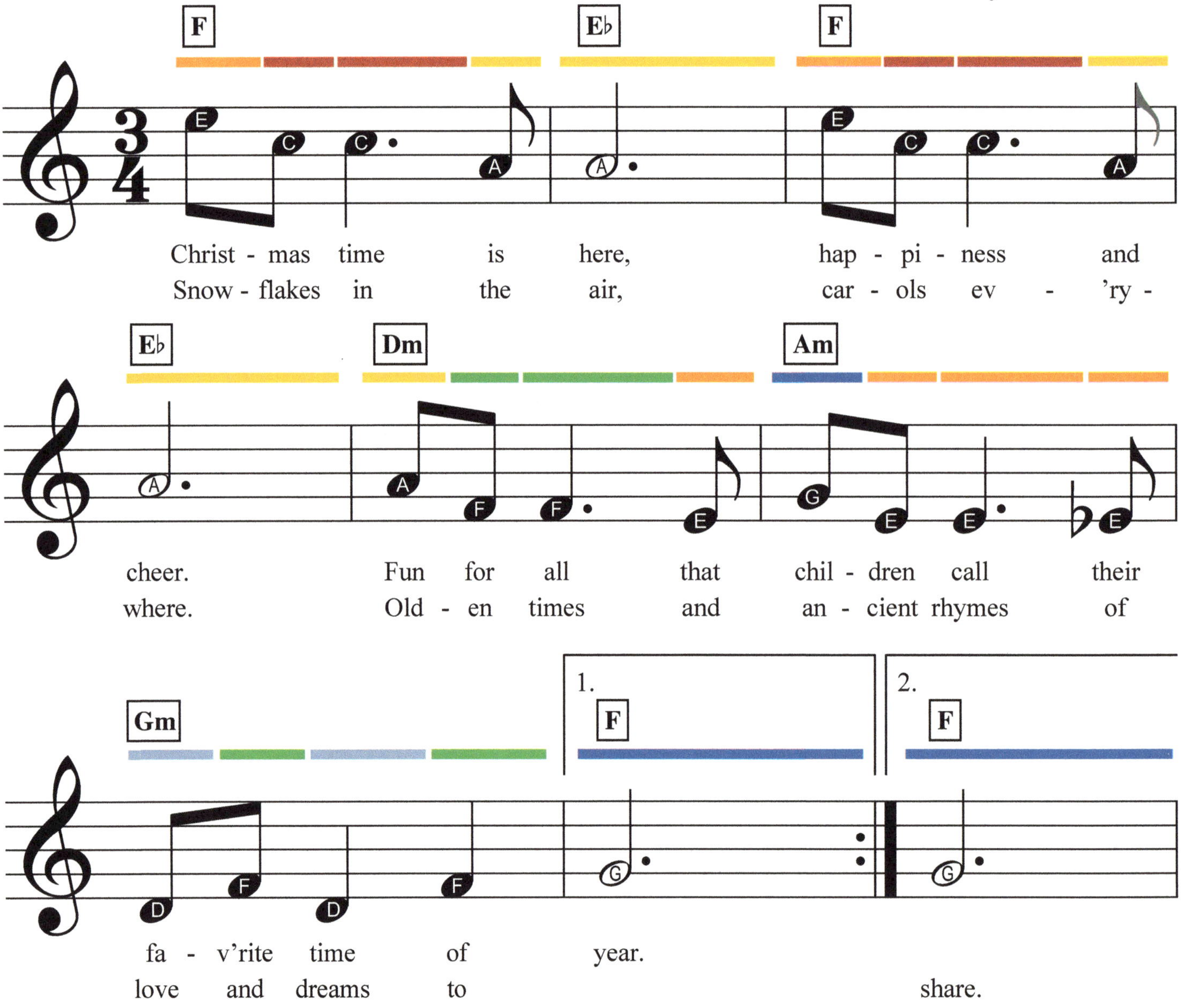

| F | E♭ | F |

3/4 E C C. A | A. | E C C. A

Christ - mas time is here, hap - pi - ness and
Snow - flakes in the air, car - ols ev - 'ry -

| E♭ | Dm | Am |

A. | A F F. E | G E E. E

cheer. Fun for all that chil - dren call their
where. Old - en times and an - cient rhymes of

| Gm | 1. F | 2. F |

D F D F | G. | G.

fa - v'rite time of year.
love and dreams to share.

Copyright © 1966 LEE MENDELSON FILM PRODUCTIONS, INC.
Copyright Renewed
International Copyright Secured   All Rights Reserved

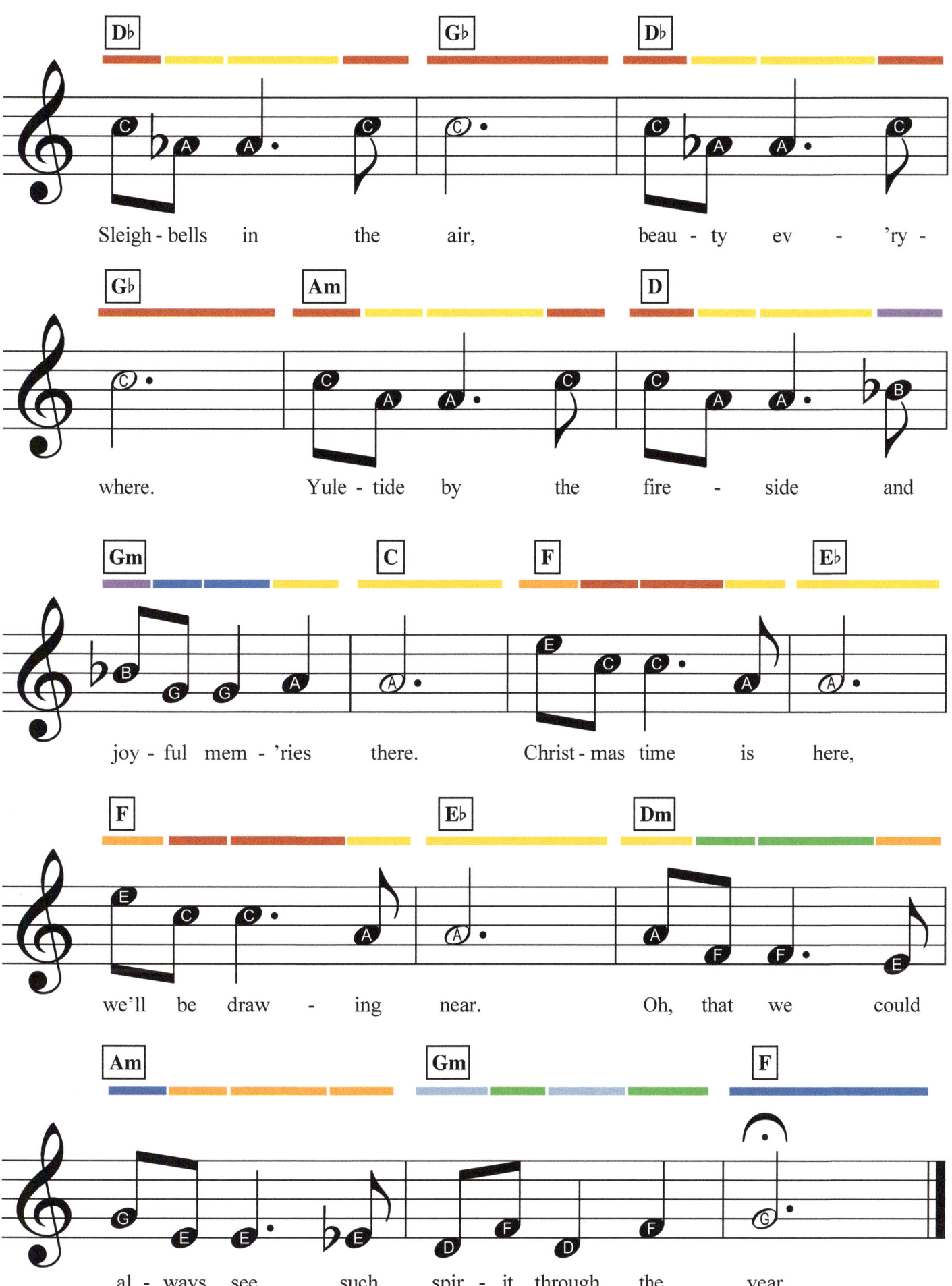

Maze Fun

Help Snoopy find Woodstock.
How many different paths can he take?

O TANNENBAUM

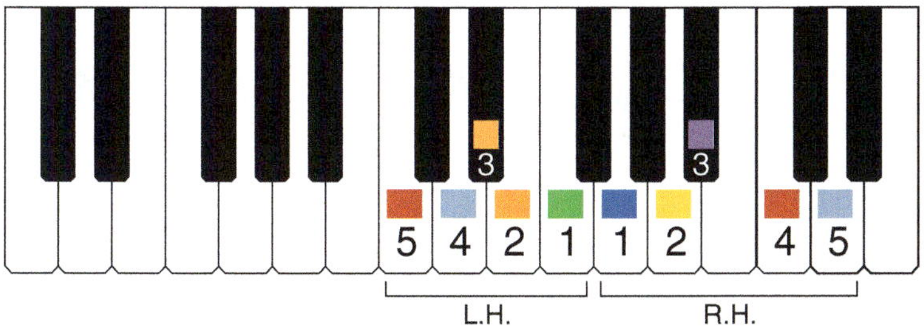

from A CHARLIE BROWN CHRISTMAS
Traditional
Arranged by Vince Guaraldi

Copyright © 1966 LEE MENDELSON FILM PRODUCTIONS, INC.
Copyright Renewed
International Copyright Secured   All Rights Reserved

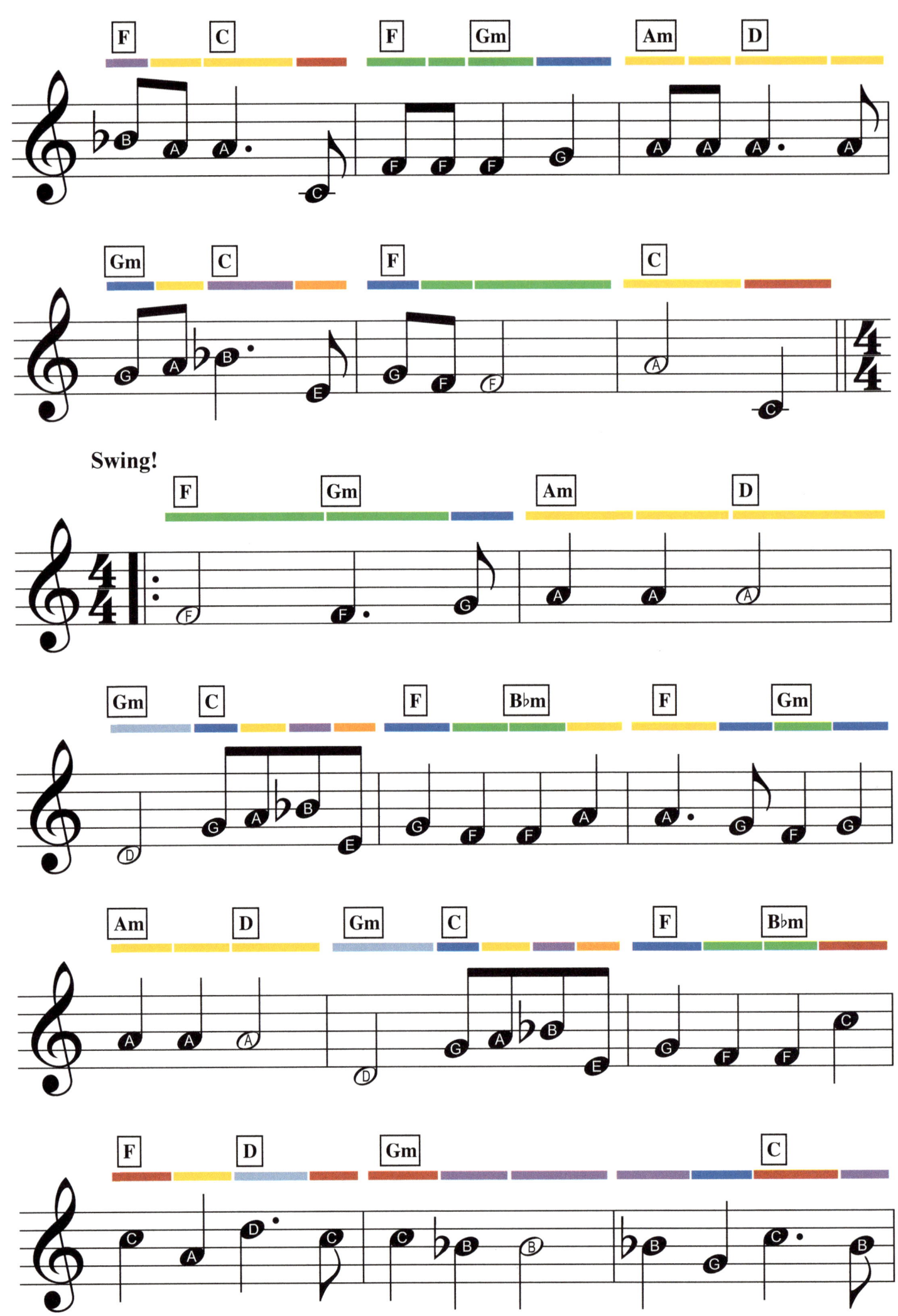

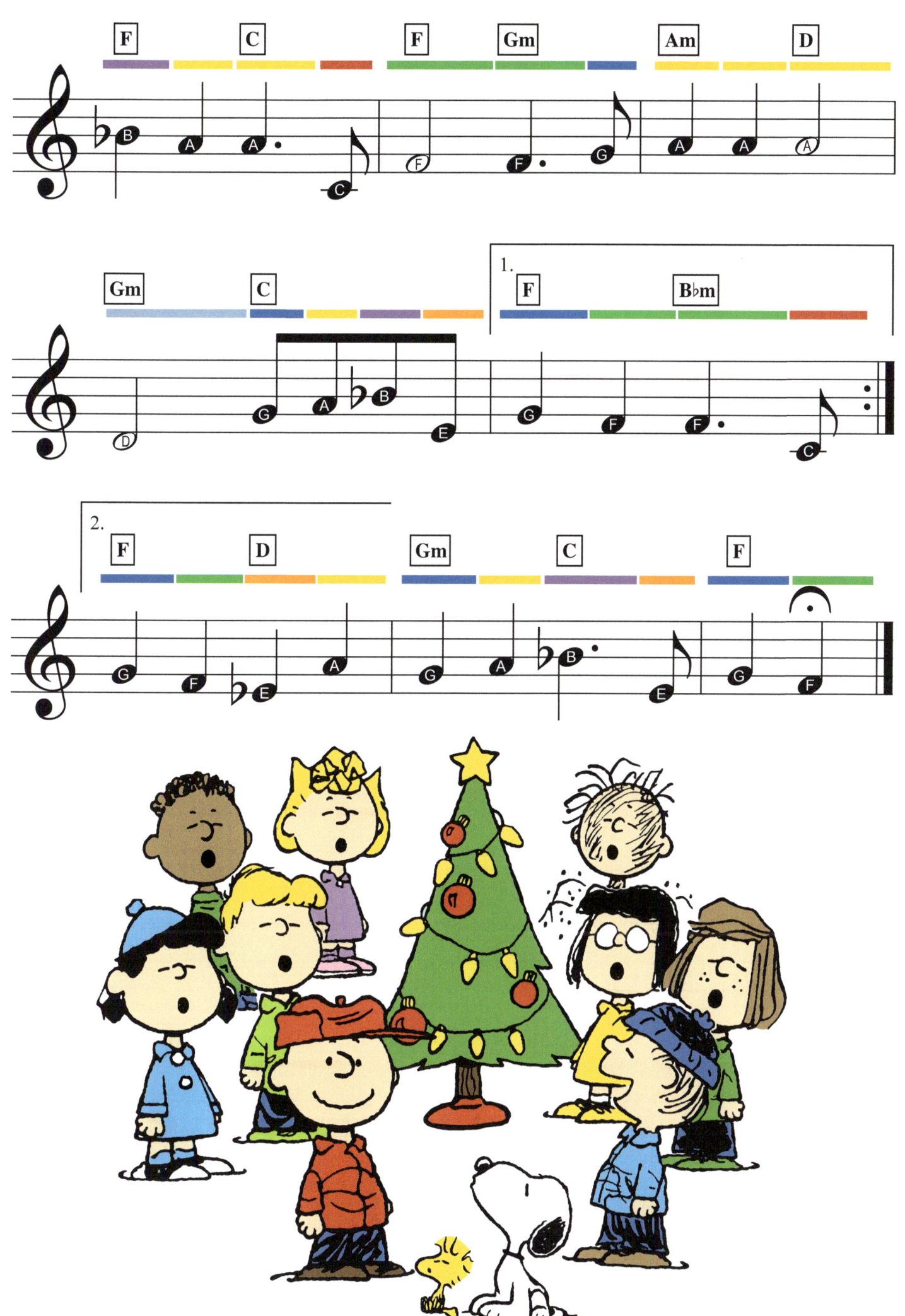

Triplets

A triplet divides a quarter note into 3 equal parts.

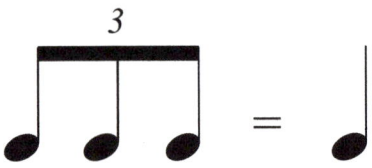

Count triplets "1 + a"

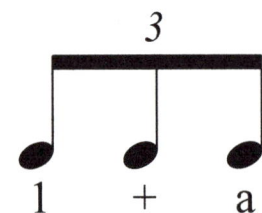

Notice how easily you can see the beats when there are several triplets in a row.

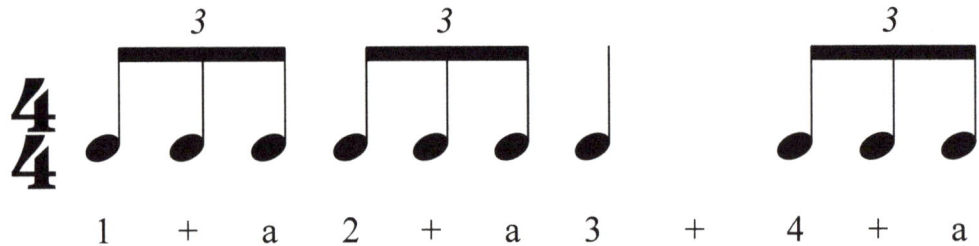

Practice triplets by clapping and counting the rhythms below.

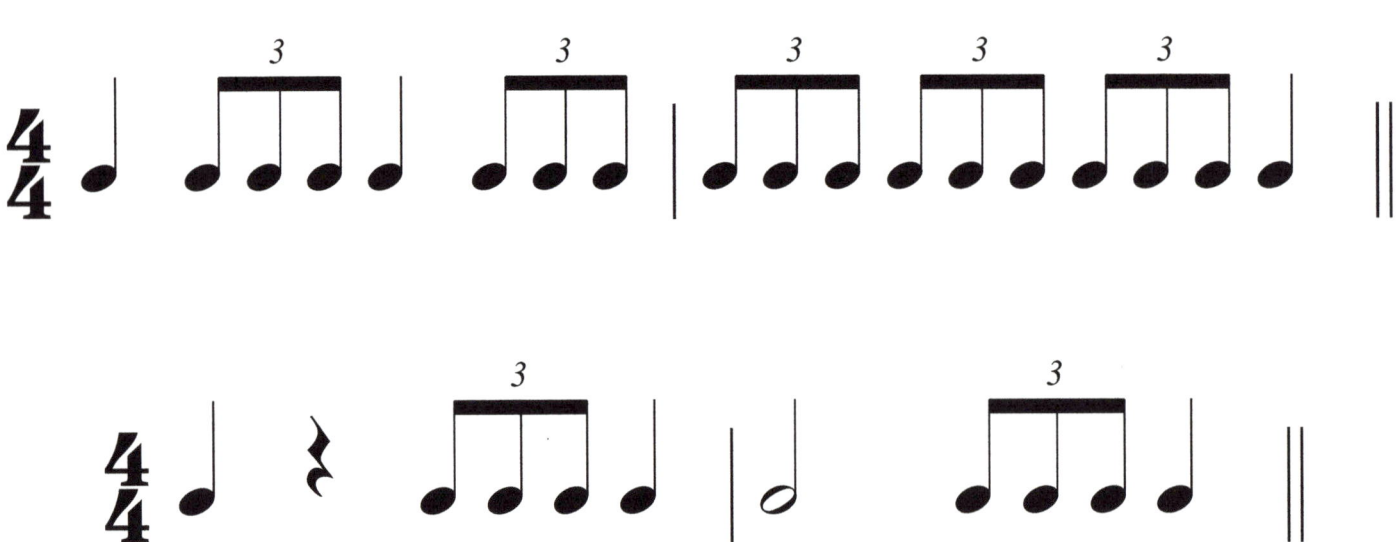

Complete the measures below. Use at least one triplet in each example.

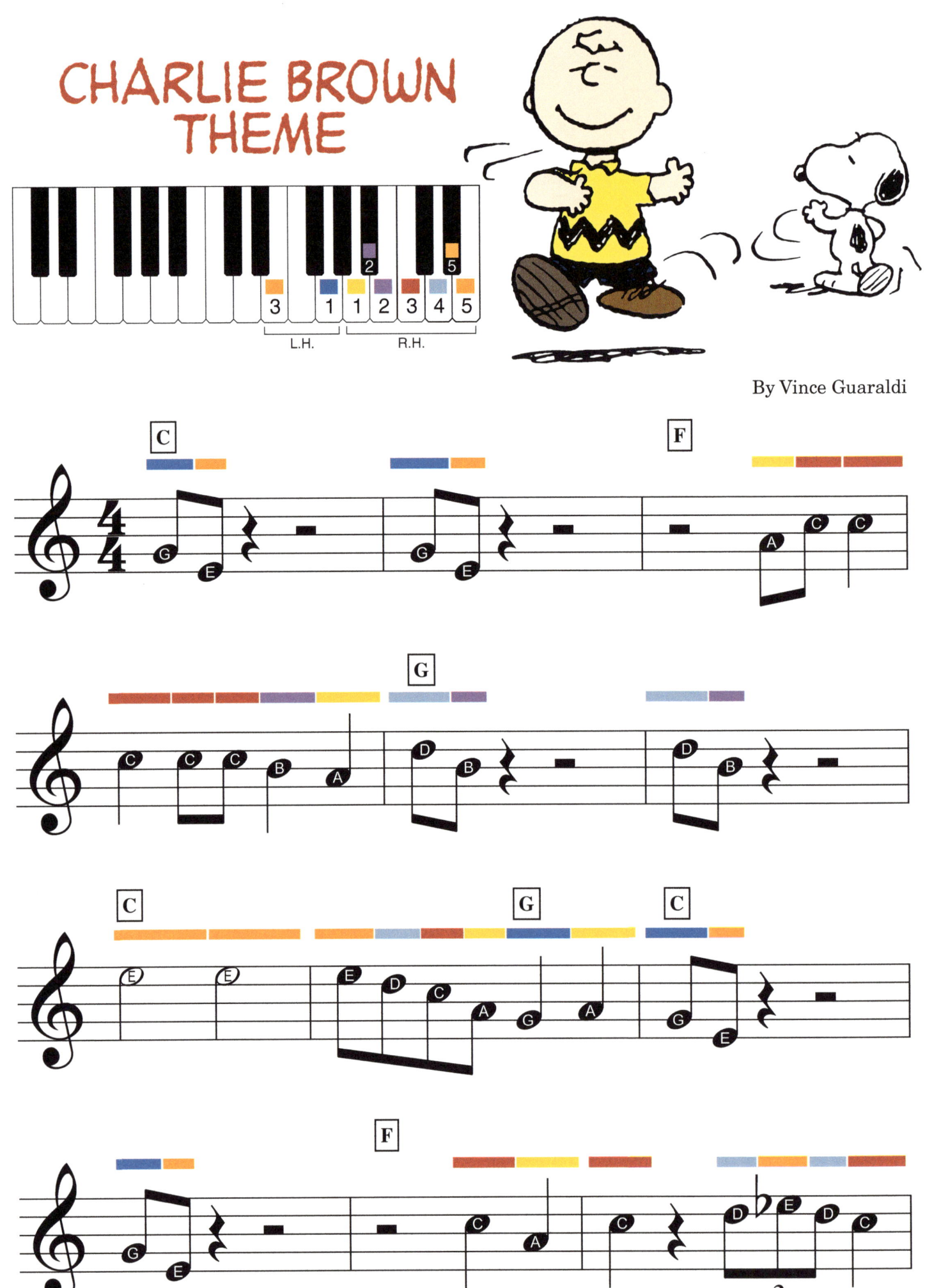

THE GREAT PUMPKIN WALTZ

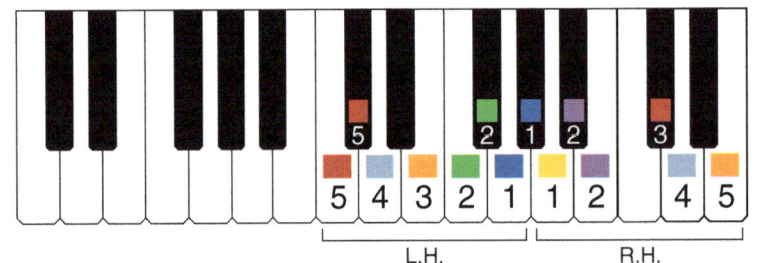

By Vince Guaraldi

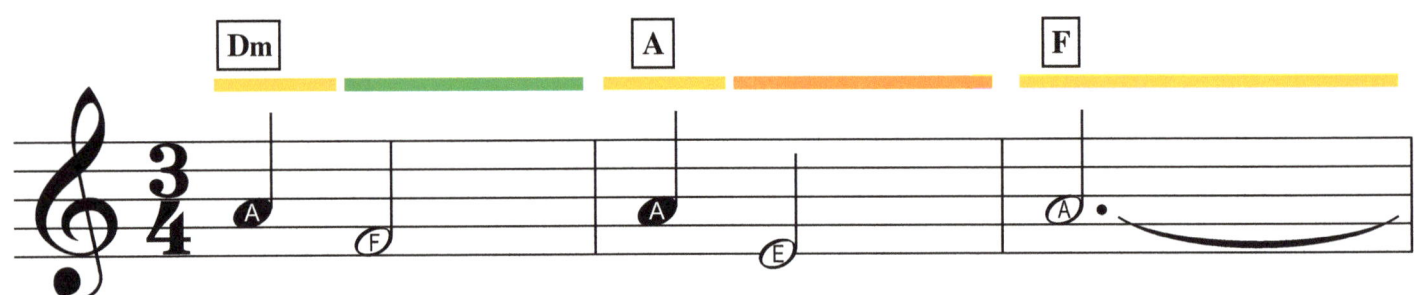

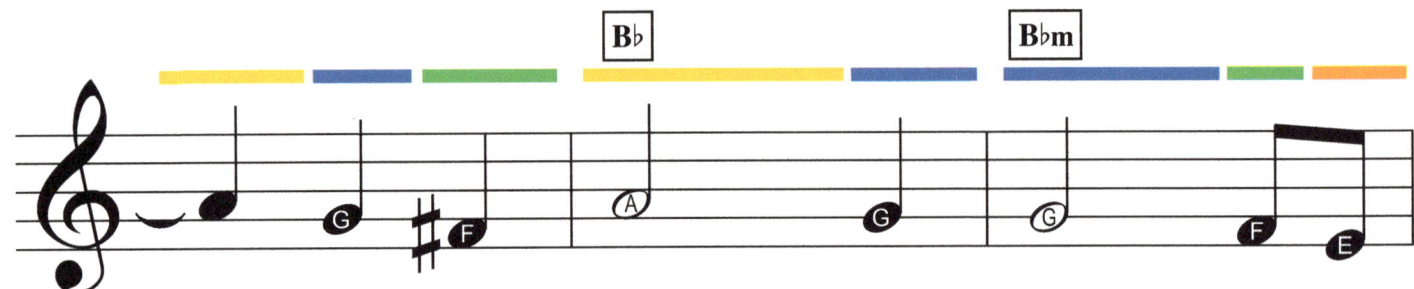

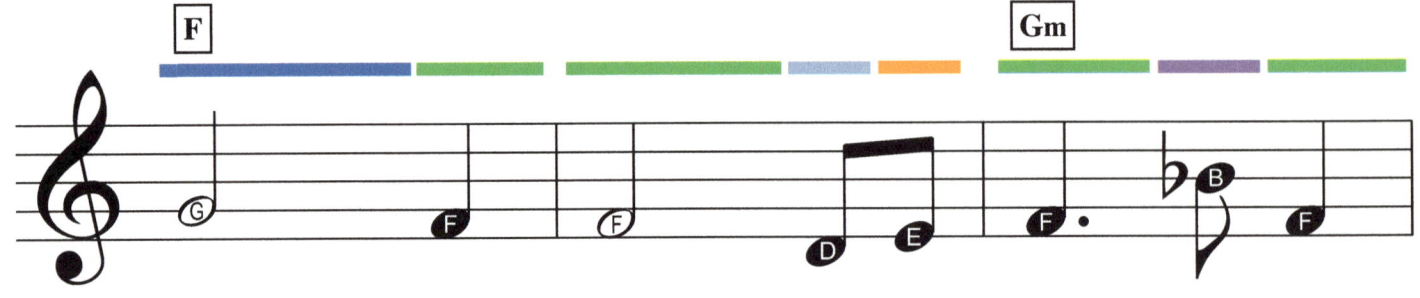

Copyright © 1969 LEE MENDELSON FILM PRODUCTIONS, INC.
Copyright Renewed
International Copyright Secured   All Rights Reserved

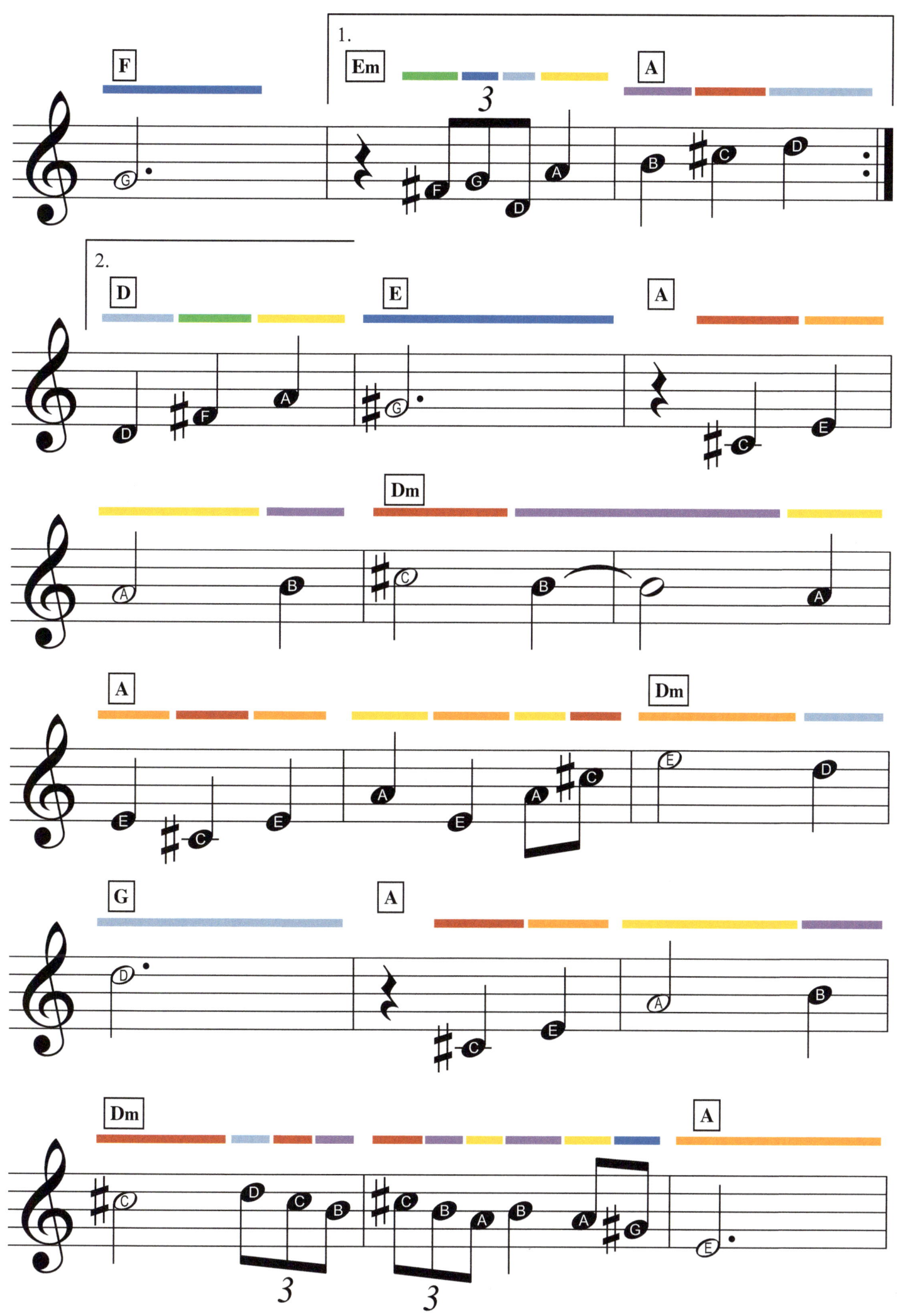

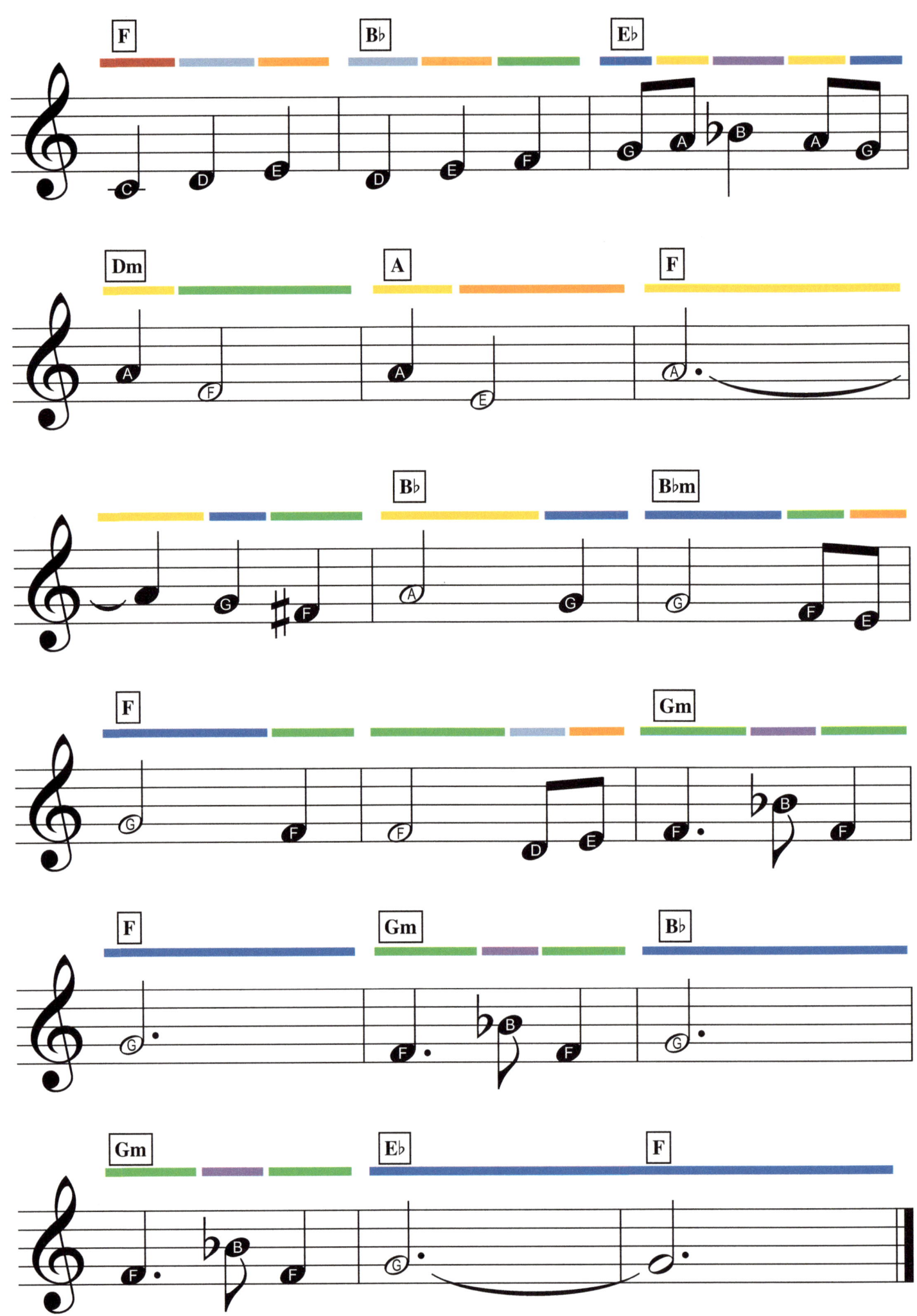

Triplet Fun

Look carefully at this picture of Snoopy and the Beagle Scouts.
Find the hidden triplets and circle them.

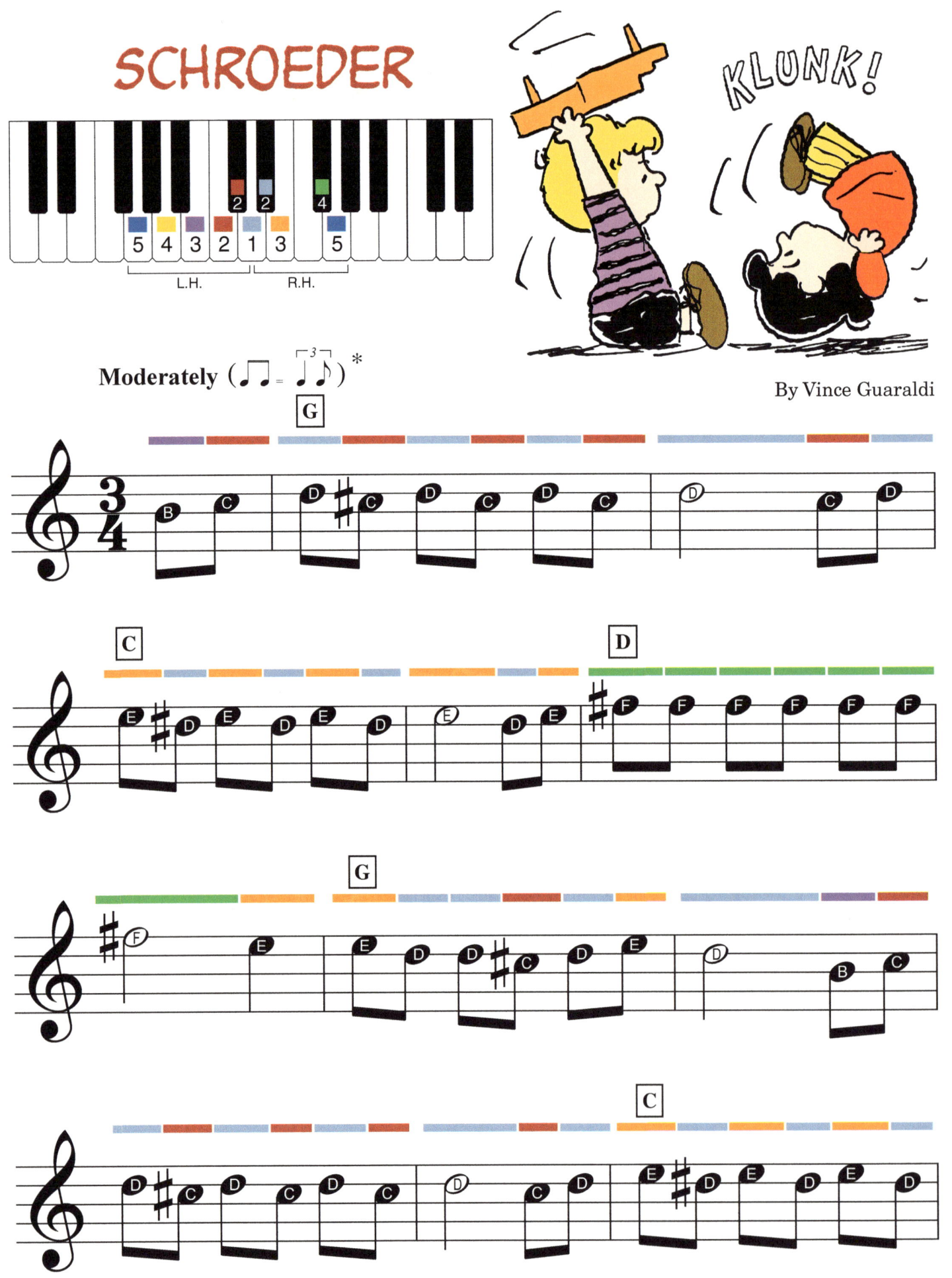

FÜR ELISE

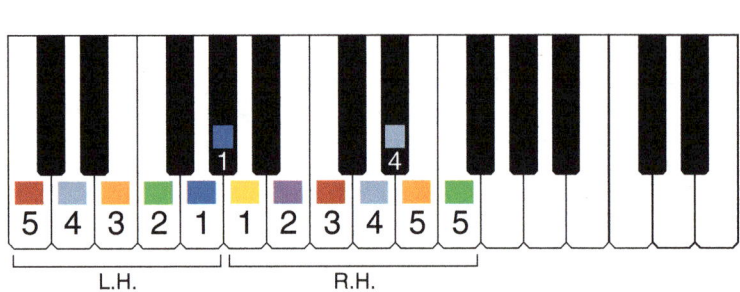

from A CHARLIE BROWN CHRISTMAS
By Ludwig van Beethoven
Arranged by Vince Guaraldi

Moderately

Syncopation

In many rhythm patterns, the strongest beat occurs on the first beat of the measure.

In $\frac{4}{4}$ time, the strong beats fall on one and three.

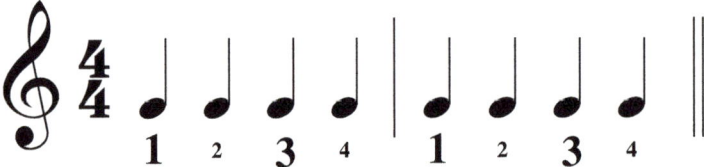

When beats other than these receive a strong accent, we hear *syncopation*. Syncopation in music is when an accent occurs on what is usually a weak beat in the measure. One of the most common syncopated rhythms is when an eighth note is played on beat one, followed by a quarter note.

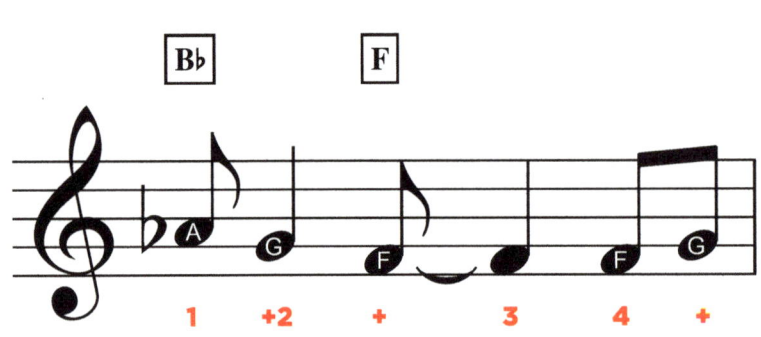

Sometimes syncopation occurs when a note is tied.

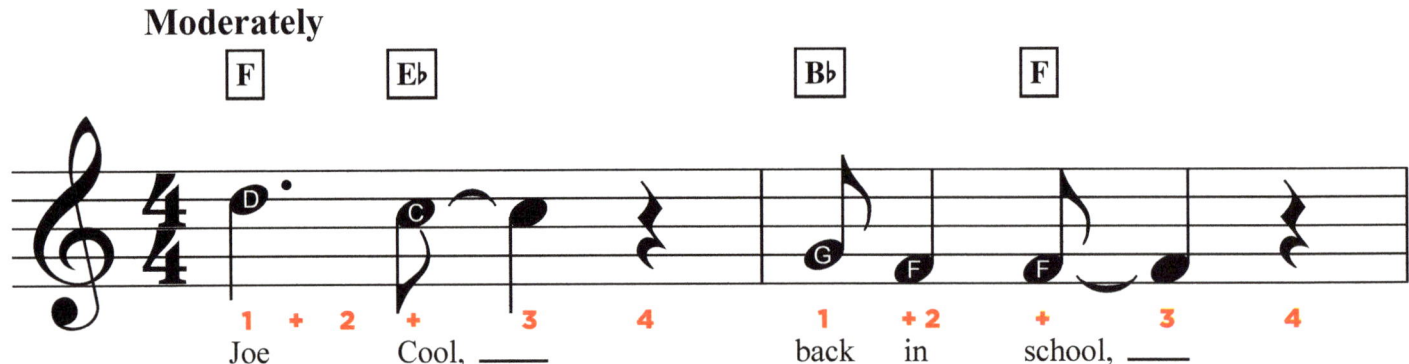

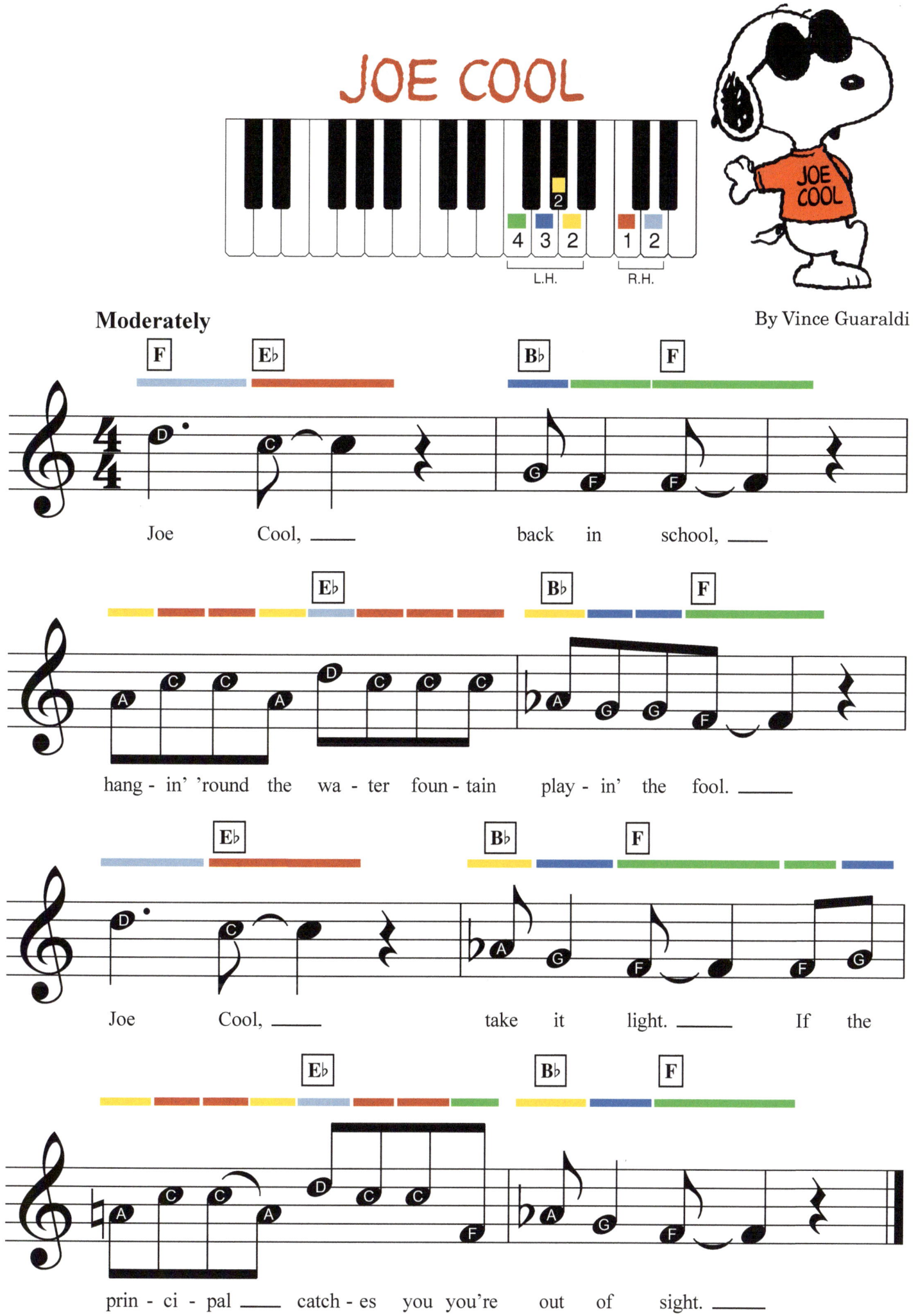

Word Search

Can you find all the music words on the list? Circle the words you find and then cross them off the list as you work.

```
K Q H D A C A P O Y Q D A S B T I W L V K Q H
E K V O O Z S T G B X C M W O X R G E P X X Z
Y E V P R M W P L H A H C H Q J Z I I E X W O
B L J T E M P O A Z R O Y O M J B T T B B Q I
O U B B B W S I Y C P R V L G G G O H A F C X
A D T S N U Q T D N E D X E K V N I Q R R R Y
R Y E U K U B C X O G S T N R D F Z O L E M L
D N B I Z I F O C T G Y Q O E K B S O I S F M
C A O R G W P S K E I M H T X C A P S N T M M
B M T A F H L I T S O B T E E C H K B E T U S
D I Y R O B T U H U H O P X O L L Q U S H S O
I C L A E E H H S T D L X T I P T I C A H I W
Q S O R B B S U N H L E D G E R L I N E A C S
U F B S G S L M L O A B G M D K V G K E L A T
A H P A C T B E F T T R I E D G O M K F F L A
R O L L O E E X C P C E P A O F I Y V T N P F
T F M R D P A P C L E K F S U V D M U P O H F
E B B P A G M K S Q E L I U B U Q G T W T A Z
R E P E A T S I G N Z F N R L H Z A N Z E B S
N O S D A P A L H P V N E E E A L W M F H E C
O U V H X T Y F S C A L E J B F Z T Q X S T V
T H T I E K L O L U G J R M A A S B V R T E U
E T I M E S I G N A T U R E R C Y J R T L I Q
```

Arpeggio	Dynamics	Measure	Skip
Bar lines	Eighth note	Music alphabet	Space
Beam	Fine	Notes	Staff
Beat	Flag	Quarter note	Step
Chord symbol	Flat	Repeat sign	Tempo
Coda	Half note	Rest	Tie
Da capo	Keyboard	Rit	Time signature
Dotted note	Ledger line	Scale	Treble clef
Double bar	Line	Sharp	Whole note

Answers on page 96.

D.C. al Coda

A new kind of repeat is used in "Skating" on page 84. At the bottom of page 86 there is the direction, *D.C. al Coda*. D. C. stands for *Da Capo*, which means to go back to the beginning of the song, and *Coda* is an ending measure or section. After you return to the beginning of the song, play until you see the direction "To Coda," and then jump to the section marked Coda, playing until the end of the song.

Dynamics

Dynamics are symbols for how softly or loudly the music will be played. Most of the words are in Italian. Here are some common dynamics, and what they mean.

>*piano* ***p*** = soft
>*forte* ***f*** = loud
>*mezzo piano* ***mp*** = medium soft
>*mezzo forte* ***mf*** = medium loud

There are other symbols in music that help you play expressively. One of those symbols is *rit.,* which is short for *ritardando*, meaning to slow the music slightly. You'll often see this at the end of a song, like in "Skating." Slow the music slightly to bring the song to a gentle ending. Tempo markings tell us about the speed and character of a song. These are found at the beginning of the song, right above the time signature.

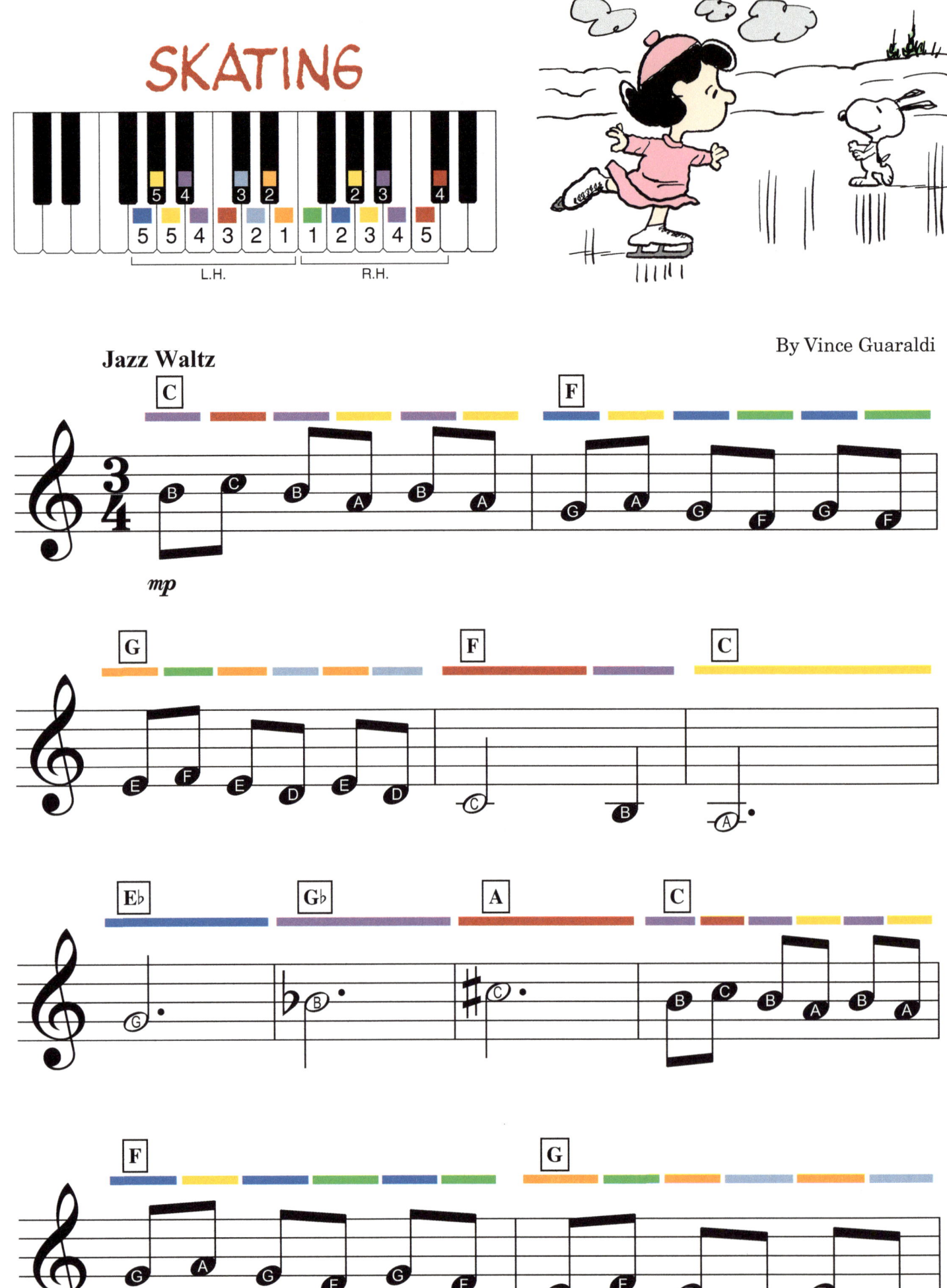

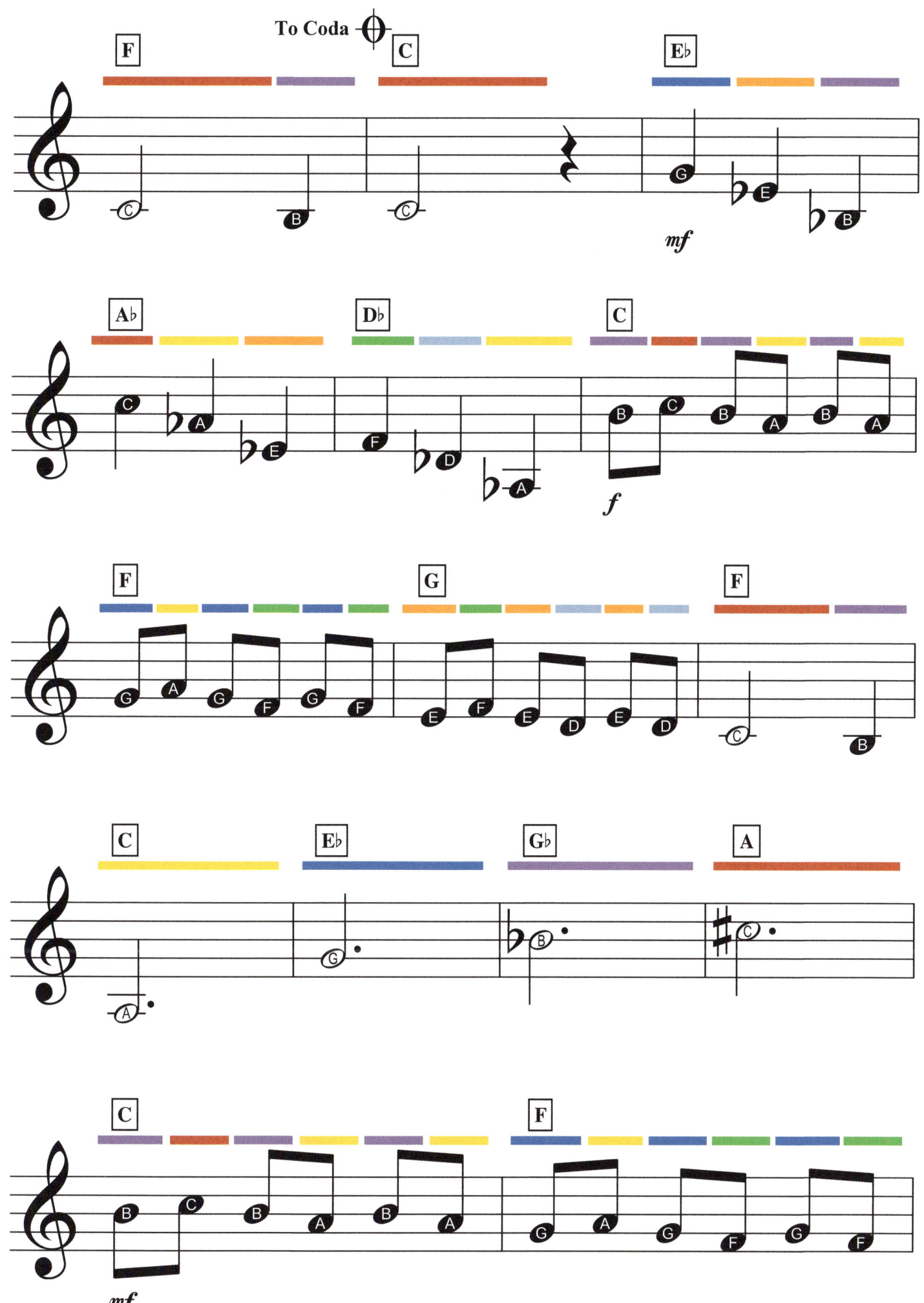

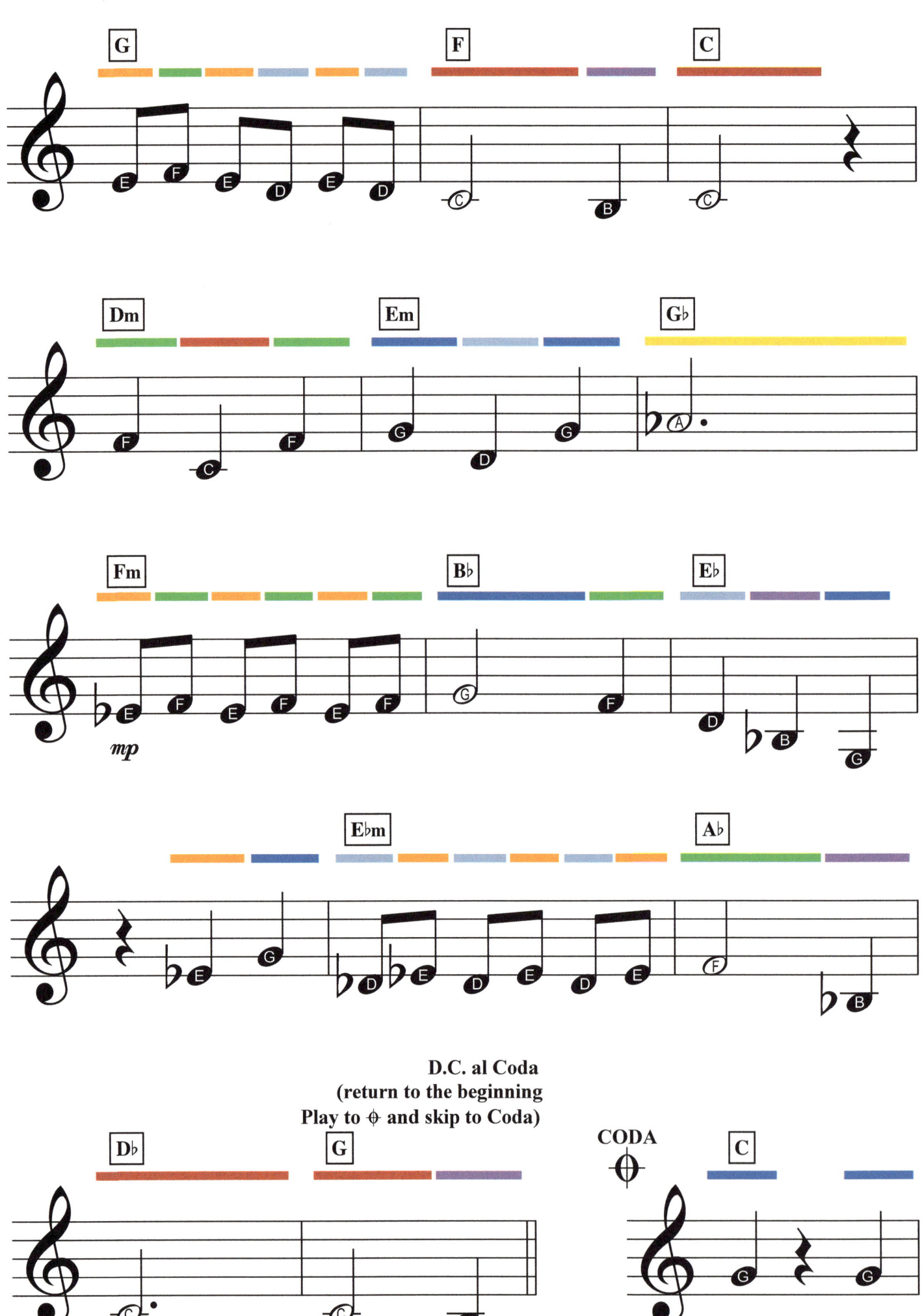

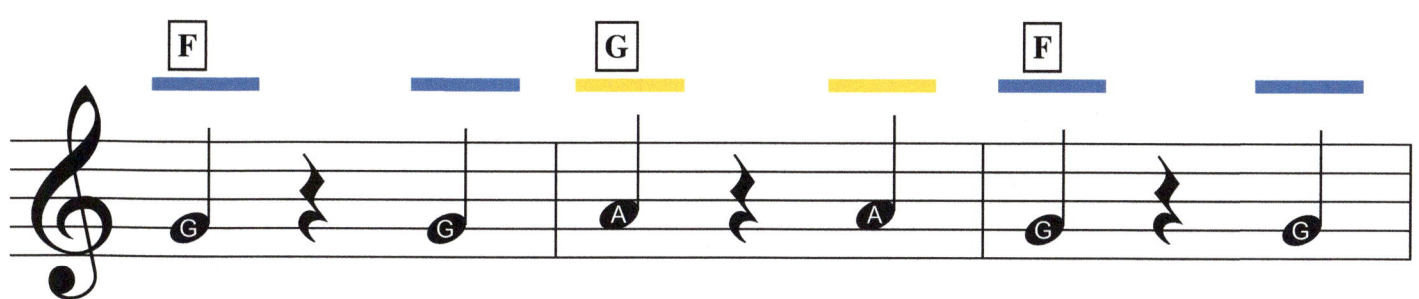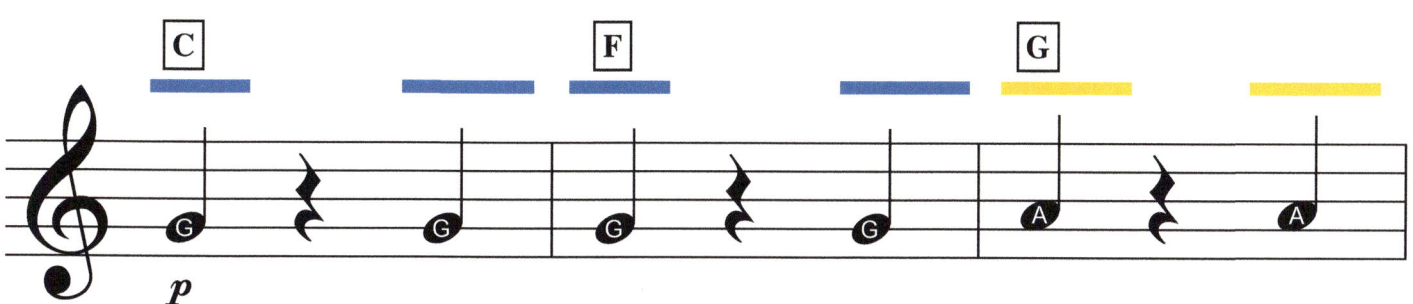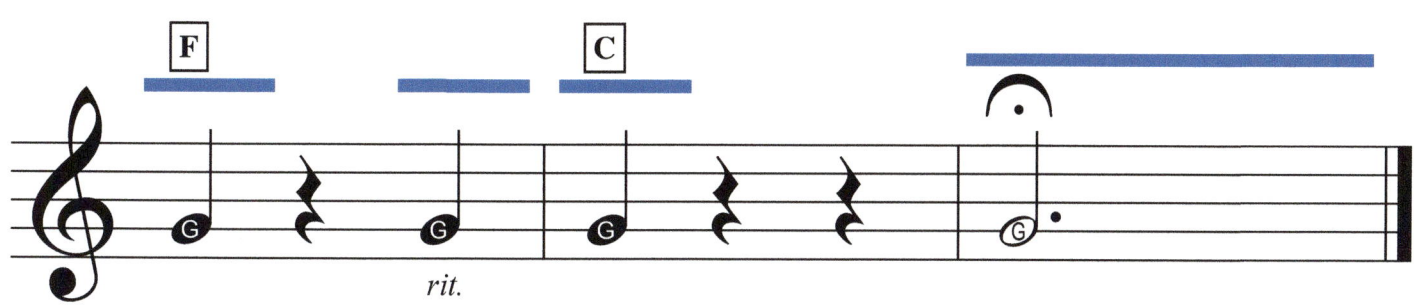

# HOUND DOG

Moderate Shuffle Words and Music by Jerry Leiber and Mike Stoller

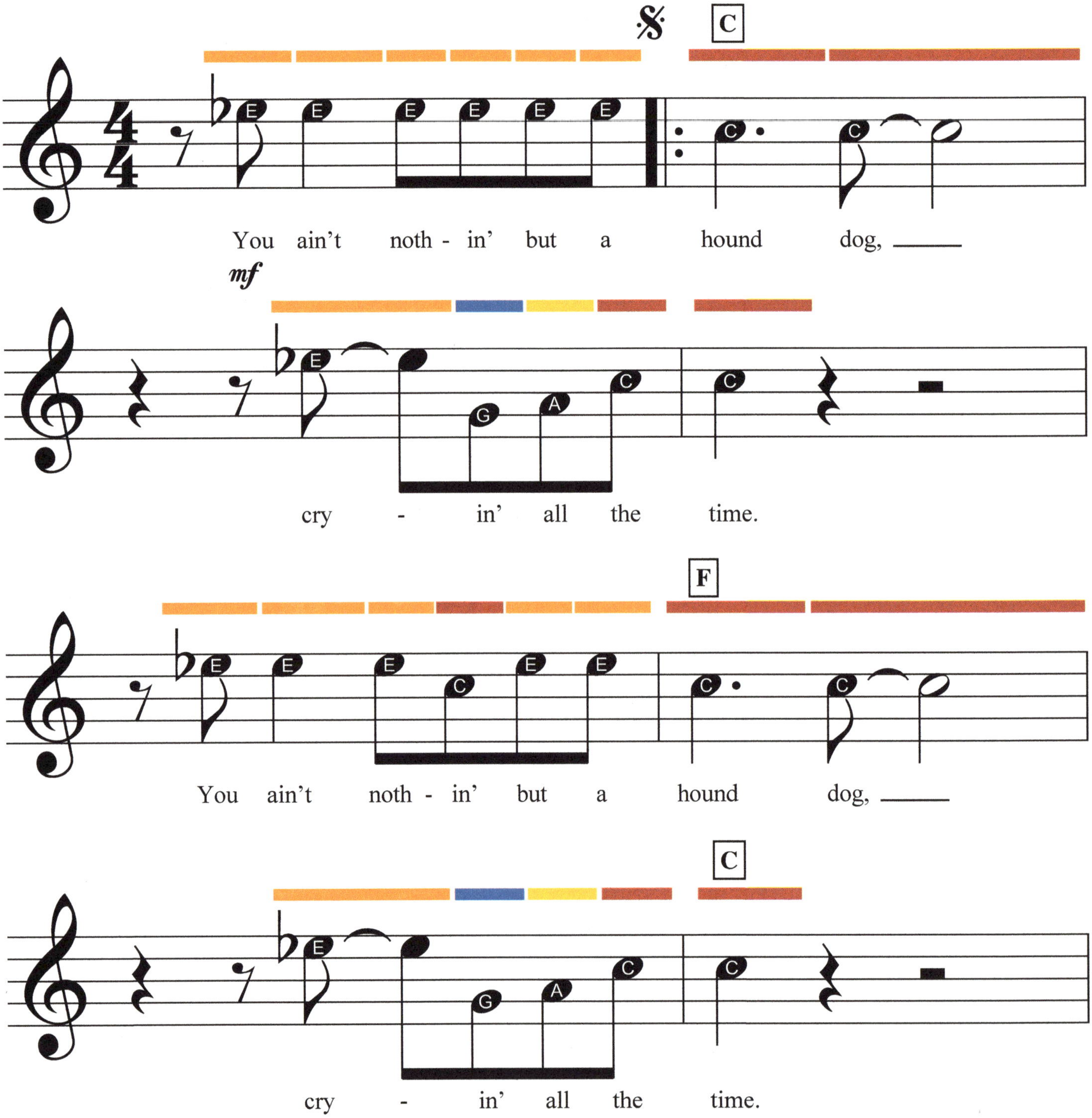

You ain't noth-in' but a hound dog, _____ cry - in' all the time.

You ain't noth-in' but a hound dog, _____ cry - in' all the time.

Copyright © 1953 Sony/ATV Music Publishing LLC
Copyright Renewed
All Rights Administered by Sony/ATV Music Publishing LLC, 424 Church Street, Suite 1200, Nashville, TN 37219
International Copyright Secured   All Rights Reserved

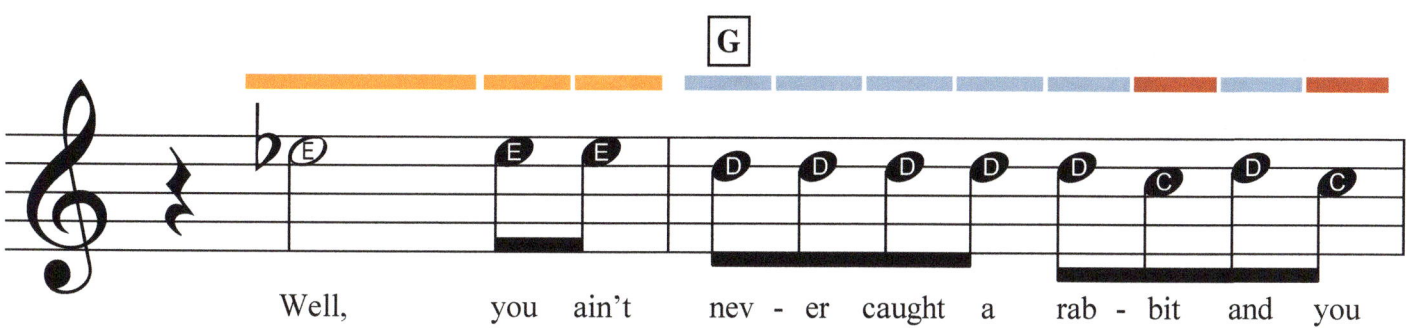
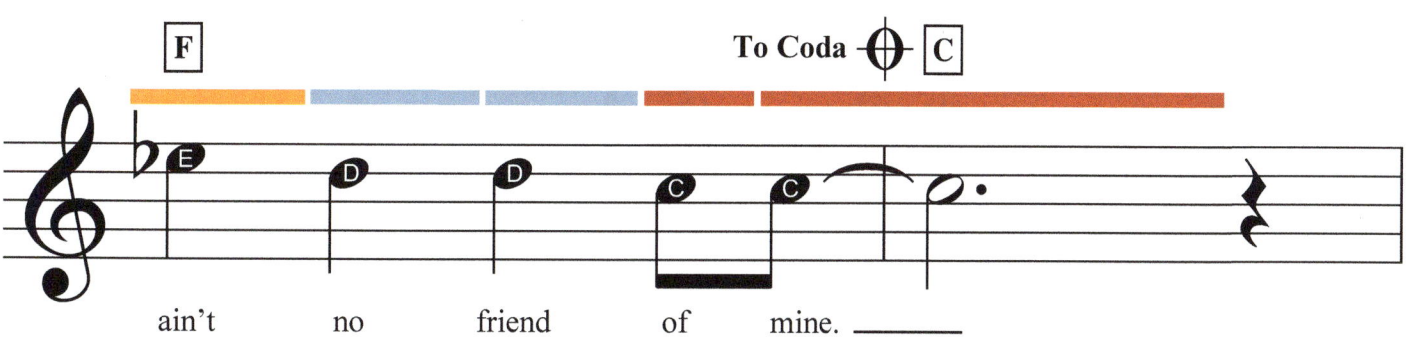
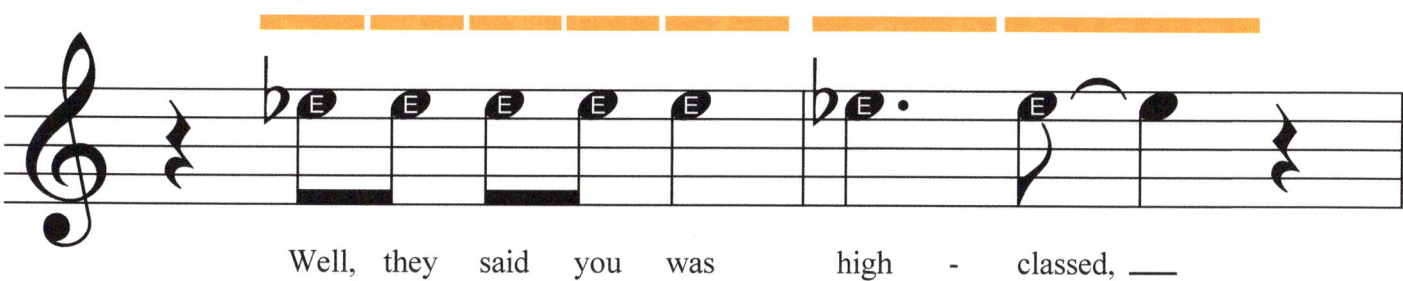
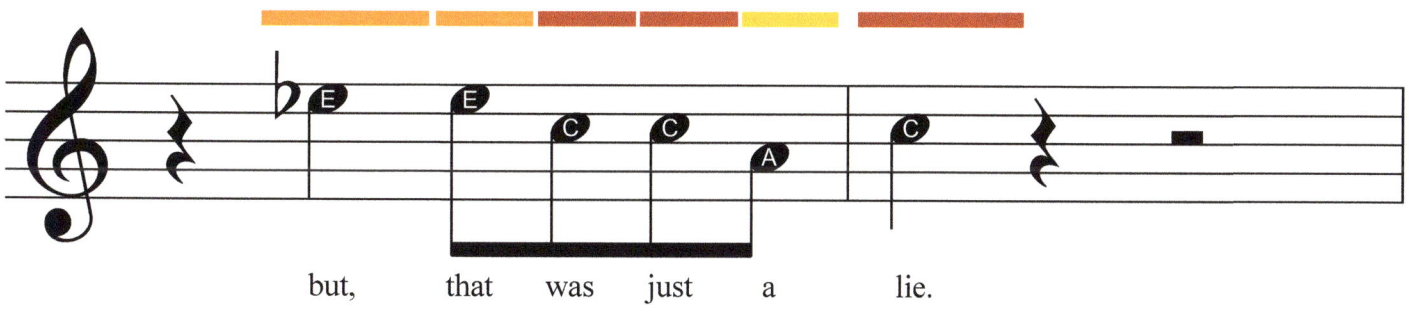
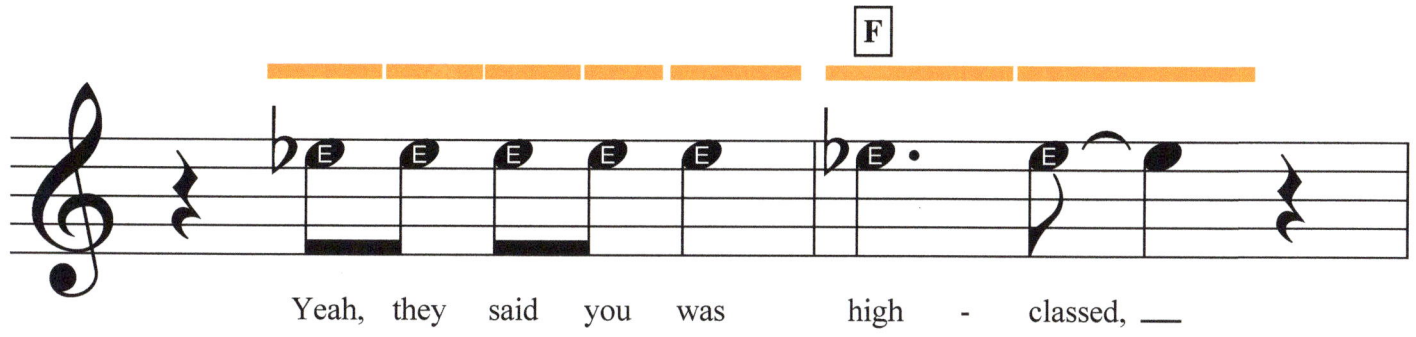

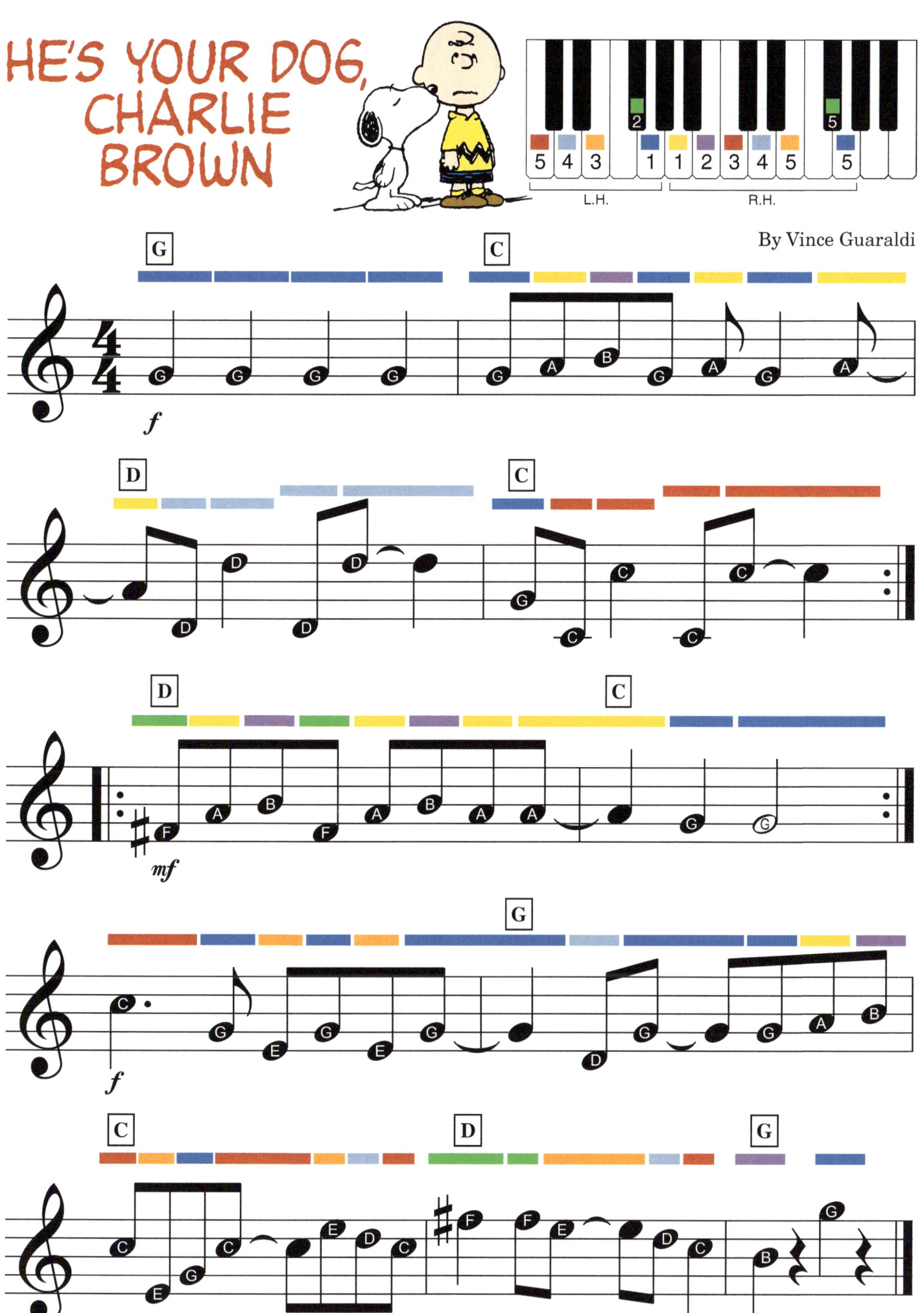

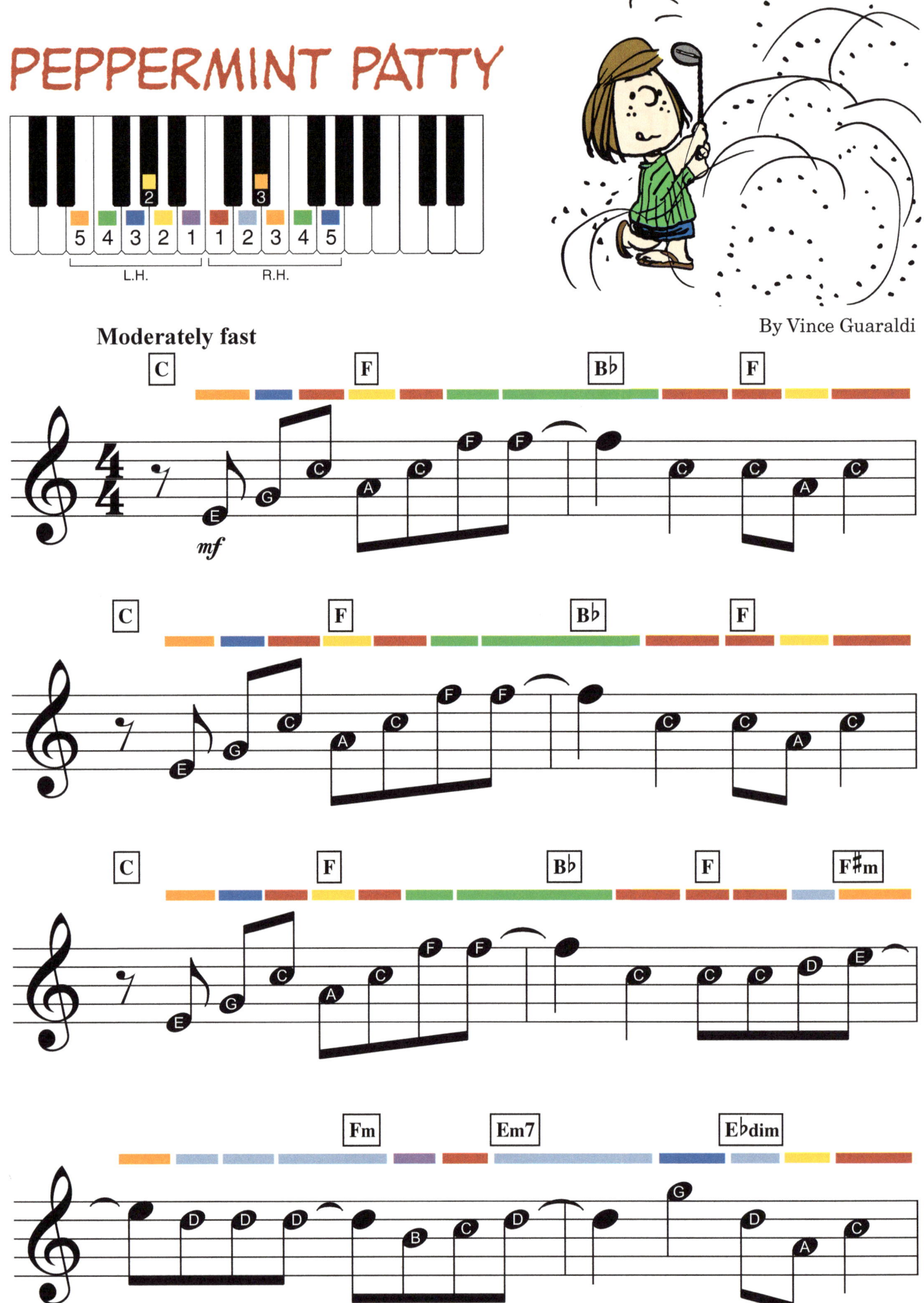

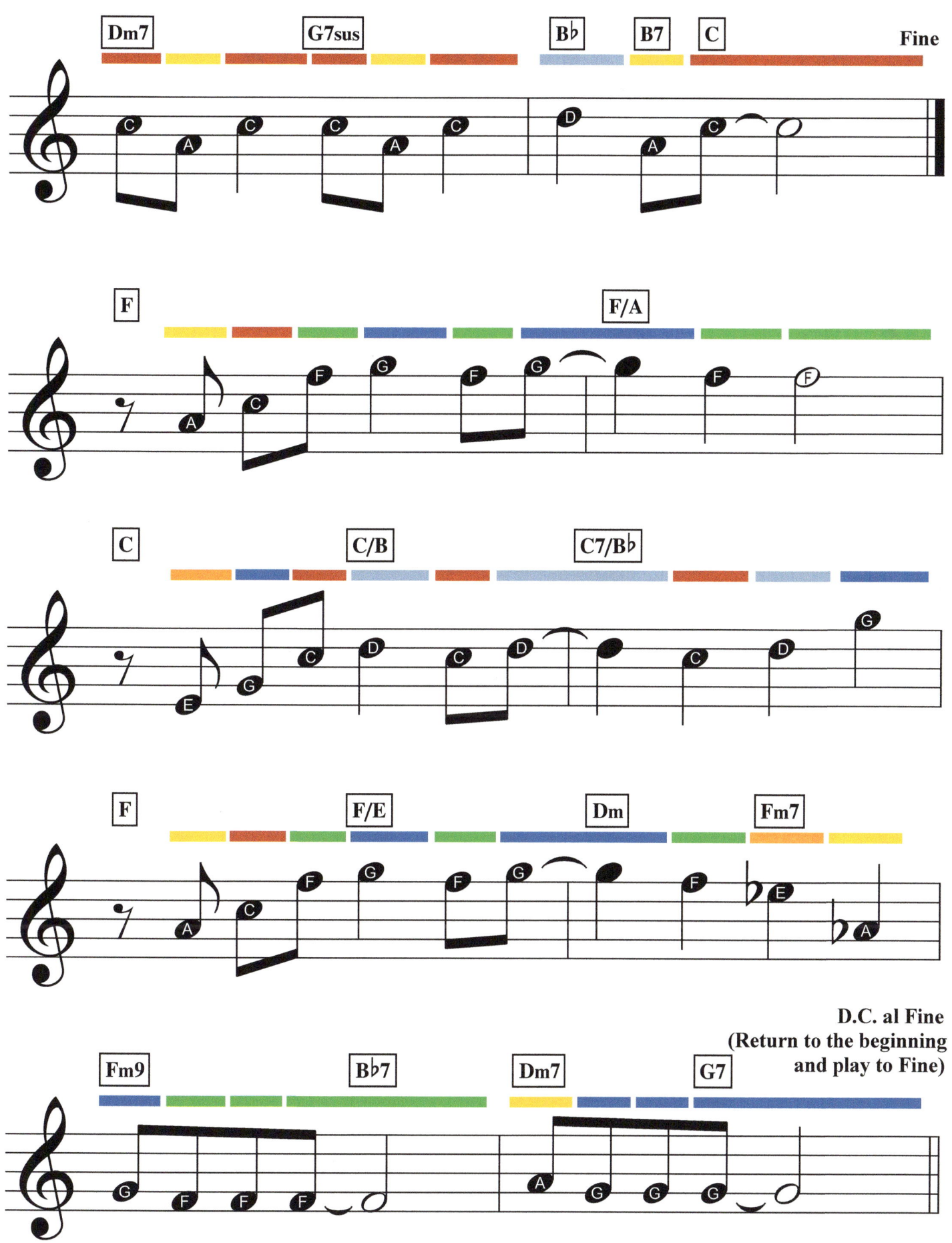

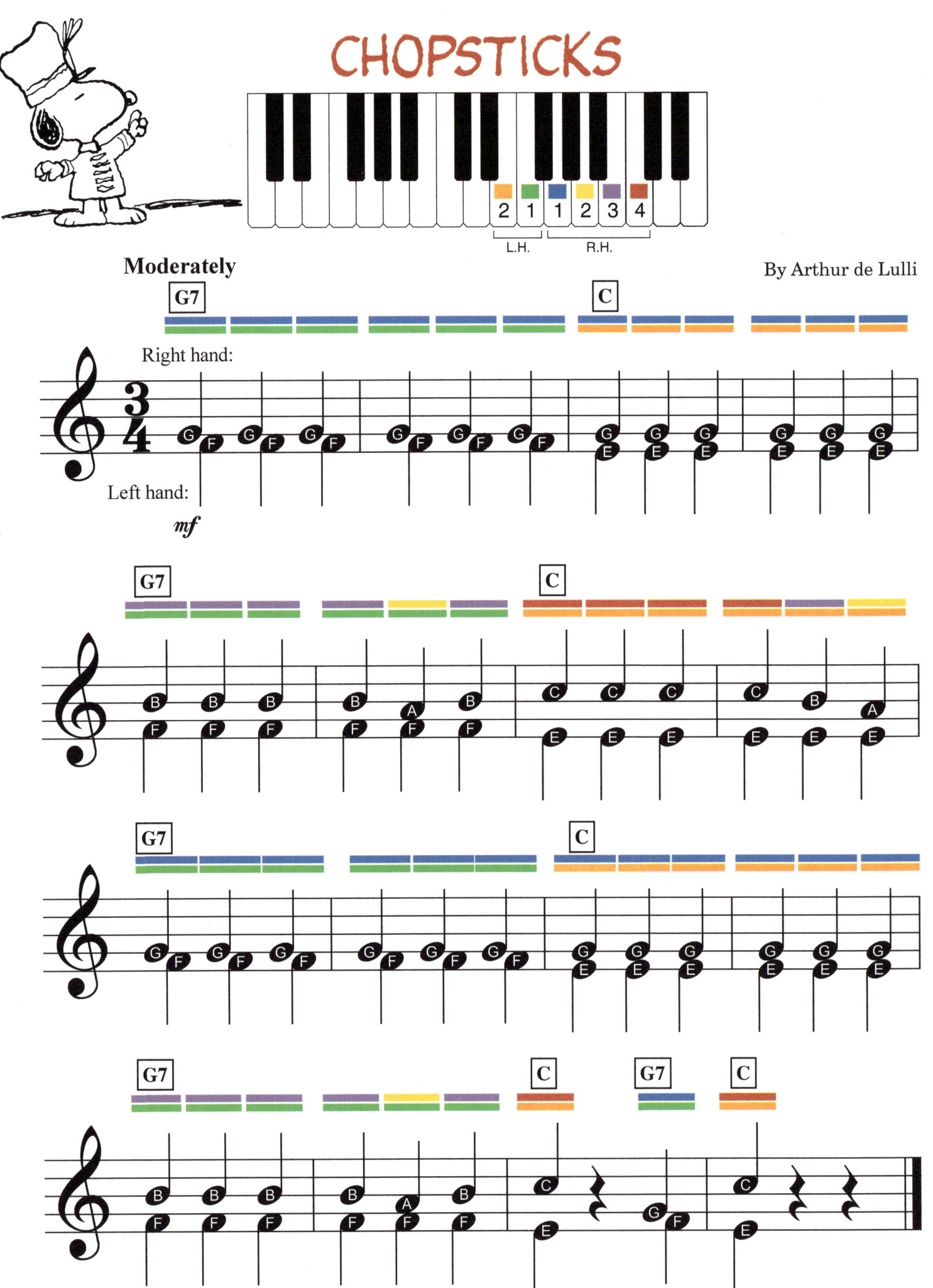

Duet Part (Solo plays one octave higher than written.)
   Moderately

Answer Key

p. 22

p. 26
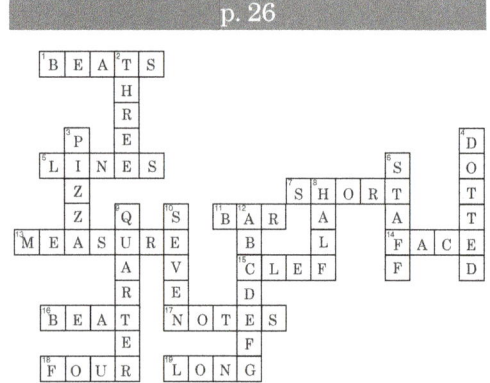

p. 31
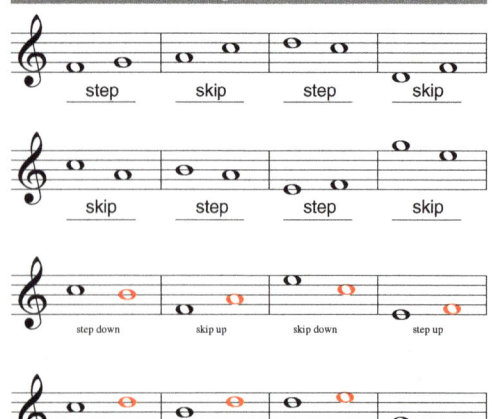

p. 33

p.38
1.) F♯
2.) D♭
3.) A♭
4.) C♯
5.) E♭
6.) D♯
7.) E♭
8.) B♭
9.) F♯
10.) G♯

p. 43
2.) 1 + 1 + 1 = 3
3.) 2 + 2 = 4
4.) 4 + 1 + 2 = 7
5.) 4 + 2 = 6
6.) 1 + 4 = 5
7.) 4 + 1 + 1 = 6
8.) 4 + 4 = 8
9.) 1 + 1 + 1 + 1 = 4
10.) 2 + 2 + 2 + 2 = 8

p. 49
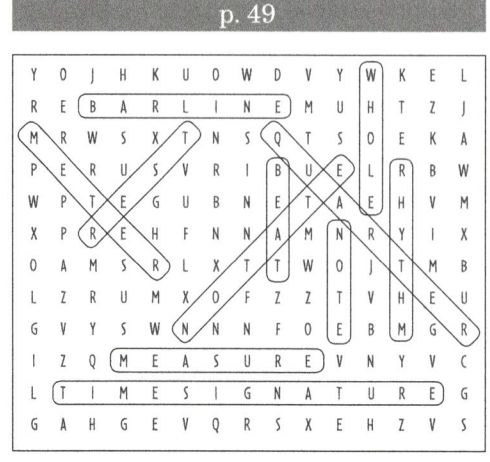

p. 49
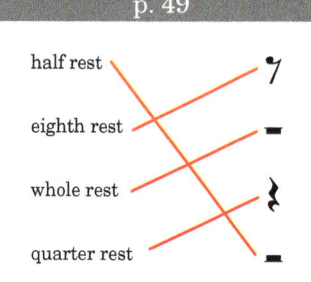

p. 59
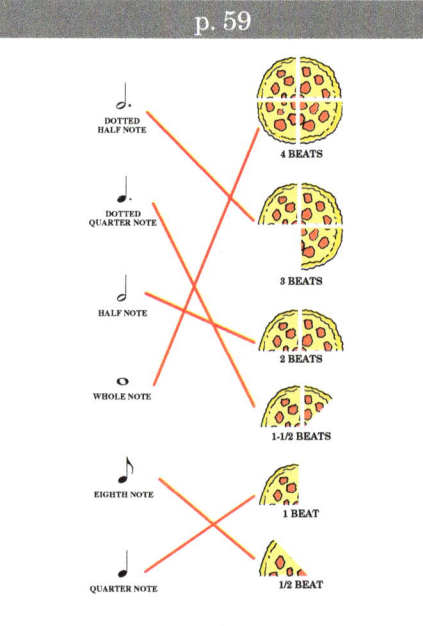

p. 82
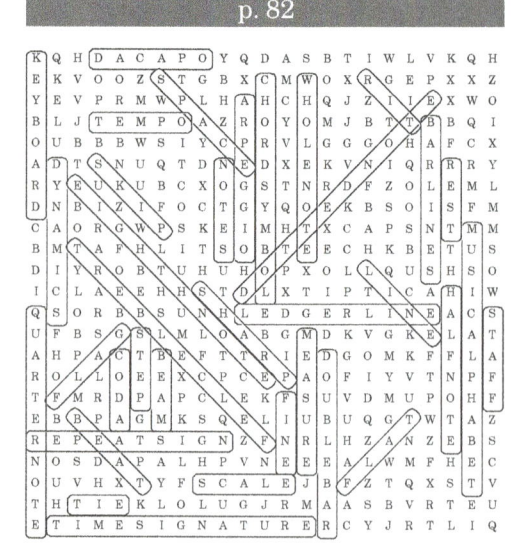